THE UNHAPPINESS
OF BEING
A SINGLE MAN

FRANZ KAFKA

THE UNHAPPINESS OF BEING A SINGLE MAN

Essential Stories

Edited and translated from the German
by Alexander Starritt

PUSHKIN PRESS
LONDON

Pushkin Press
71–75 Shelton Street
London WC2H 9JQ

This translation first published by Pushkin Press in 2018

1 3 5 7 9 8 6 4 2

ISBN 13: 978-1-78227-439-1

Frontispiece: Franz Kafka and dog, around 1905
© Pictorial Press Ltd / Alamy Stock Photo

Designed and typeset by Tetragon, London
Printed and bound in Great Britain by TJ International,
Padstow, Cornwall on Munken Premium White 80gsm

www.pushkinpress.com

Contents

Translator's Preface

IN ENGLISH, the word that usually follows 'Kafkaesque' is 'nightmare'. Hardly the thing to make you think, 'Hurray, a new translation. No Netflix for me tonight.' And in truth, Kafka's work is respected far more than it is loved.

Potential book buyers sense that reading one of his novels might be unpleasantly similar to appearing in it: boring and painful at the same time. Like a circle of hell reserved for bureaucracy and anxiety dreams, where you fill in meaningless forms until the end of time, and then discover the pen is actually a beetle. That feeling only gets stronger when you flick to the back of *The Castle* and see how many pages there are.

I can't say I really disagree. There's no question about how startling Kafka's vision is, nor about how, despite the surrealism and the grotesquerie, it all feels so familiar. But are the novels a great read? I have my doubts.

Not so about the short stories. There, the ideas that can feel interminable in the novels are quick, funny, strange and sad. Some are fables, some are jokes, some seem placid at first then throw you out the window, some put pictures in your mind that no one but Kafka ever could and that will keep resurfacing for years afterwards as metaphors for your lived reality. Some you read and think, oh I see, *this* is Kafka, this is why Kafka was such an earthquake, this is why he's unforgettable.

Just to be blunt: I think the short stories you hold in your hand are the best thing Kafka ever wrote, and the best of them are as good as anything ever written by anyone. If you don't want to take my word for it, on the back of my German edition it says, "The short stories form the actual core of all Kafka's work."

So why are they less known than the novels? I think it's probably because people tend to buy novels rather than short story collections, and therefore publishers tend to push them. Kafka's short stories have often appeared in unwieldy compendia, aimed at devotees, or appended to an edition of his most famous piece, *The Metamorphosis*.

Translation also creates an extra cost that makes it harder for publishers to take the gamble on an unpopular form. And although Kafka has had some excellent translators, like Michael Hofmann, in many editions you see the marks left by the economics of publishing: underpaid translators work quickly and hurry to get things finished.

I hope this collection takes these short stories out from under the novels' shadow. I haven't put them in chronological order, or tried to showcase his different modes; my principle for inclusion has been: only the best.

A MESSAGE FROM
THE EMPEROR

T HE EMPEROR—they say—has sent you, you alone, his lowly subject, you tiny shadow thrown far off into the furthest corner by the imperial sun, you, of all people, the Emperor has sent a message from his death-bed. He had his messenger kneel down beside him and whispered the message directly into his ear; it was so important to him that he had the message repeated back into his own. With a nod he confirmed that what had been said was correct. In front of the entire audience of his death—every obstructing wall had been torn down and the great and good of the empire were gathered around, crowding onto the sweeping staircases that led up to him—in front of them all he sent the messenger on his way. The messenger, a strong, a tireless man, set off at once; pushing himself forward arm over arm, he clears a path through the crowd; if someone blocks his way, he points to the symbol of the sun emblazoned on his chest; and he gets through faster than anyone else ever could.

But the crowd is so big; there's no end to them and their city. If he could get onto the open road, he'd be flying along, and soon you'd hear the wonderful hammering of his fists on your door. But how futile his efforts are; he's still fighting his way through the apartments of the innermost palace; he'll never make it out of them; and even if he did, nothing would be gained; he'd still have to fight his way down the staircases; and even if he did that, nothing would be gained; he'd still have to cross the courtyards; and after the courtyards the second, outer palace; and again staircases and courtyards; and then another palace; and so on through thousands of years; and if finally he burst out of the outermost gate—but never, never can that happen—he'd still have the whole imperial capital ahead of him, the centre of the world, its buildings piled high and its streets clogged up. Nobody can push through that, least of all carrying a message from a dead man. — But you sit at your window and dream of what it says, when evening comes.

A SHORT FABLE

"Ach," said the mouse, "the world gets narrower every day. At first it was so wide it was frightening; but I kept running and I was glad when I finally saw some walls far off to the left and right of me, but now those long walls are hurrying towards each other so fast that I'm already in the final room, and there in the corner is the trap I'm running into." — "All you have to do is run in the other direction," said the cat, and ate it.

THE UNHAPPINESS OF
BEING A SINGLE MAN

IT SEEMS A TERRIBLE THING to stay single for good, to become an old man who, if he wants to spend the evening with other people, has to stand on his dignity and ask someone for an invitation; to be ill and spend weeks looking out of the corner of your bed at an empty room; always to say goodbye at the door; never to squeeze your way up the stairs beside your wife; to live in a room where the side doors lead only to other people's apartments; to carry your dinner home in one hand; to be forced to admire children you don't know and not to be allowed to just keep repeating, "I don't have any"; to model your appearance and behaviour on one or two bachelors you remember from childhood.

That's how it's going to be, except that in reality both today and in the future you'll actually be standing there yourself, with a body and a real head, as well as a forehead, which you can use your hand to slap.

POSEIDON

P OSEIDON SAT at his desk and went through his accounts. Being in charge of all the seas and oceans was an endless amount of work. He could have had assistants, as many as he wanted, and indeed he did have very many of them, but because he took his position very seriously, he checked over every calculation again himself, and so his assistants were little help to him. You couldn't say that the work gave him pleasure; he actually just did it because it had been assigned to him. In fact he'd often asked for some work that would be what he called a bit more cheerful, but whenever suggestions were made to him it turned out that nothing suited him as well as the position he already had. It was also very difficult to find something else for him. It would have been impossible to appoint him to a particular sea, for example. Even leaving aside that the amount of bookkeeping would have been no smaller, merely pettier, the great Poseidon could of course only be given a role at a very senior level. And if he was offered something outside the water altogether, just the idea of it made him ill, his divine breathing grew laboured and his powerful ribcage started to heave. Also, his complaints weren't taken very seriously; when a powerful person starts fretting, you have to look like you're trying to help them no matter how pointless the matter at hand; but no one ever really thought that Poseidon would be allowed to resign his position. He'd been appointed god of the seas at the beginning of time and that's the way things would have to stay.

What annoyed him most—and this was mostly due to dissatisfaction with his work— was when he heard about what people imagined he was like, for example that he was always careening through the waves with a trident. Meanwhile he was sitting down here in the depths of the ocean constantly going through the books. The only interruption to this monotony were occasional visits to Jupiter, visits, by the way, from which he usually returned in a fury. So he'd hardly seen anything of the seas, only ever briefly on the hurried ascent to Olympus, and never really travelled around them. He would say that he was waiting for the end of the world; at that point there would surely be a quiet moment before it was all over in which, after finishing off the last of the accounts, he'd have time for a quick look around.

THE VERDICT

A story for Ms Felice B.

I**T WAS A SUNDAY MORNING** at the height of spring. Georg Bendemann, a young businessman, was sitting in his room on the first floor of one of those low, straightforwardly built houses that run in a long line beside the river, differing from each other only in their height or colour. He'd just finished writing a letter to a childhood friend and folded it shut with whimsical attentiveness, then, resting his elbows on the desk, he looked out of the window at the river, the bridge and the pale green hills on the other bank.

He was thinking about how this friend, dissatisfied with the way his life was going at home, had all but fled to Russia several years ago. These days he ran a business in St Petersburg, which had got off to a very good start but now seemed to have been stagnating for some time, something the friend complained about on his increasingly rare visits. He was fruitlessly working himself into the ground in a far-off country, his foreign-looking beard only patchily covering his familiar face, which was developing a yellowish tinge that hinted at some emerging illness. From what he said, he didn't have any real connections out there among the expatriate community, nor much social contact with Russian families, and so was preparing himself for permanent bachelorhood.

What could you write to a man like that, who had obviously made the wrong choices, someone you could sympathize with but not help? Should you maybe advise him to come home, to move his life back here, to take up all his old friendships again—there was no reason he couldn't—and in general to put his trust in the fact that his friends would help him? But doing that would be tantamount to saying—and the more gently it was put, the more hurtful it would be—that all his efforts so far had failed, that he should finally let it go, that now he had to come back and let himself be stared at by everybody who knew he'd come back for good, that his friends had known better than him what to do with their lives and that actually he was just an overgrown child who should concentrate on imitating those who'd made a success of staying where they were. And was is it even certain that all the pain he'd have to go through would be worth it? Perhaps they wouldn't even be able to convince him to come back—he said himself that he didn't understand his home country any more—and in that case he'd stay

abroad despite everything, embittered by his friends'
advice and alienated even further from them. Whereas if
he did take the suggestion to come back and then ended
up downtrodden at home—of course not on purpose, but
just because it turned out like that—if he couldn't get on
with his friends or get by without them, found himself
humiliated, friendless and more truly displaced than before,
wouldn't it be much better for him if he'd stayed abroad?
Could you really expect, given all these considerations,
that he'd be able to make a go of things back here?

That was why, if you wanted to keep up a correspond-
ence with him, you couldn't give him any actual news, the
kind you would unthinkingly write to even your most distant
acquaintance. His friend hadn't been home for more than
three years, offering the unconvincing explanation that it
was because of the uncertain political situation in Russia,
which apparently wouldn't permit a small businessman to
leave the country for a few weeks even while hundreds of
thousands of Russians were traipsing around all over the
world. For Georg, however, a lot had changed in those three
years. The death of Georg's mother, which had happened
about two years ago and prompted Georg and his father to
move back in together, was something he'd told his friend,
who'd expressed his condolences in a letter so dry that it
could only be because the sorrow of something like that
becomes completely unimaginable from far away. Since
that time, Georg had thrown himself more purposefully

into the family business, as he had into everything else. Perhaps it was because, while his mother was alive, his father's insistence on managing things at work had held Georg back from really taking it on as his own; perhaps it was because his father, although he did still come to the office, had now become more withdrawn; perhaps, and in fact very probably, certain far happier events had had an important role to play, but in any case, the business had made unexpected strides in these past two years, they'd had to double the staff, turnover had gone up fivefold and even greater gains were there for the taking.

The friend had no idea about this altered state of affairs. Previously, maybe the last time had been in that condolence letter, he'd tried to persuade Georg to emigrate to Russia and written at length about the opportunities there were for Georg's line of business in St Petersburg. The numbers he'd mentioned were vanishingly small compared with the level that Georg's business had already reached. But Georg hadn't wanted to tell his friend about his commercial successes at the time, and to do so retrospectively really would seem bizarre.

So Georg limited himself to writing about the meaningless happenings that drift randomly into your mind if you sit and think on a quiet Sunday. All he wanted was to avoid disturbing the image of home that his friend must have created and come to terms with during his long absence. That's how Georg ended up telling his friend about some completely uninteresting person getting engaged to an equally uninteresting girl three times in three different letters sent quite far apart, eventually piquing his friend's interest in this strange affair.

But Georg would far rather write about things like that than admit that he himself had got engaged to a Miss Frieda Brandenfeld, a girl from a well-to-do family, about a month earlier. He often spoke to his fiancée about this friend and the unusual written relationship he had with him. "So that means he won't come to our wedding," she said, "even though I've got the right to meet all your friends."

"I don't want to put him out," said Georg. "Don't get me wrong, he would probably come if we asked him, but he'd feel pressured into it and annoyed, maybe jealous of me and certainly unhappy, and afterwards he'd have to go back to Russia by himself, feeling like he'd never be able to put that unhappiness aside, let alone overcome it. By himself—do you remember how that felt?"

"But might he not hear about our wedding from someone else?"

"I can't guarantee that he won't but, given the way he lives, it's unlikely."

"If that's what your friends are like, Georg, you shouldn't have got engaged in the first place."

"Well, that's both our fault, but now we're here I wouldn't have it any other way." And when she, breathing quickly under his kisses, said, "But actually it does bother me," he thought that it might be harmless after all to tell his friend everything. 'This is who I am and he has to take me as I am,' he said to himself. 'I can't take a pair of scissors to myself and cut out a person who'd be better suited to being his friend.'

And in the long letter he wrote that Sunday morning he did indeed tell his friend that the engagement had taken place, in the following words: "I've saved the best news for last. I'm engaged to a Miss Frieda Brandenfeld, a girl from a comfortably-off family that only moved here after you left, so the name probably won't mean anything to you. I'm sure there'll be plenty of opportunity to tell you more about her, but for now just know that I'm very happy and that this changes nothing about our friendship, except that instead of having a completely normal friend you now have a very happy one. Also, in my fiancée, who sends you her love and will write to you herself soon, you now have a sincere female confidante, which is no small thing for a bachelor. I know there are all kinds of reasons that keep you from visiting us, but wouldn't my wedding be the right moment to throw all the obstacles out of the window for once? But be that as it may, don't worry about me and just do what you think is best."

With this letter in his hand Georg sat at his desk a long time, facing the window. An acquaintance walking down the alley said hello and Georg barely responded, just giving him an absent smile.

Finally he put the letter in his pocket and, leaving his room, went straight across the little hallway into his father's, which he hadn't been in for months. There was no need to, since he was constantly in his father's company at work, they had their lunch together at a local eatery every day and, although they did separate things in the evening, if Georg wasn't out with friends or visiting his fiancée, as he usually was these days, they'd sit together for a little while, each with his own newspaper, in their shared living room.

Georg was amazed by how dark his father's room was even on such a sunny morning. He realized for the first time how big a shadow was cast by the high wall on the other side of their narrow courtyard. His father was sitting by the window in a corner that had been decorated with various mementoes of Georg's late mother and reading a newspaper, which he was holding at an angle to try and compensate for some weakness in his eyes. On the table were the leftovers from his breakfast, which he seemed to have hardly touched.

"Ah, Georg!" said his father and went over to him at once. His heavy dressing gown swung open as he walked, its ends billowing around him. 'My father is still a giant of a man,' thought Georg.

"It's so dark in here," he said.

"Yes, it's dark, right enough," responded his father.

"And you've got the window shut as well?"

"I prefer it that way."

"When it's so nice and warm outside," Georg said as if carrying on with his previous comment, and sat down.

His father tidied away the breakfast dishes and put them on top of a sideboard.

"I actually just wanted to tell you," Georg went on, distractedly following the old man's movements, "that I've sent the news of my engagement to St Petersburg." He pulled the letter slightly out of his pocket and let it fall back in.

"Why to St Petersburg?" asked his father.

"My friend there, you remember," said Georg and tried to catch his father's eye. 'He's so different at work,' he thought, 'look how solid he is at home, sitting there with his arms crossed.'

"Yes. Your friend," said his father with emphasis.

"You know, Father, that at first I didn't want to tell him about my engagement. Just to be considerate, not for any other reason. You know yourself he's a difficult person. I said to myself, he might well find out from somebody else that I'm engaged, although it's hardly likely given how solitary he is—there's nothing I can do about that—but he won't hear it directly from me."

"And now you've thought it over again?" his father asked, putting the big newspaper on the window sill, his glasses on the newspaper and his hand on top.

"Yes, now I've thought it over again. If he's a good friend to me, I said to myself, then the happy news that I've got engaged should make him happy too. And that's why I stopped hesitating and told him about it. But before I post the letter, I wanted to mention it to you."

"Georg," said his father with a toothless grimace, "listen to me. You've come to me with this thing to ask my advice about it. That speaks in your favour, no doubt about it. But it means nothing, less than nothing, if you don't tell me the whole truth about it. I don't want to stir things up that shouldn't come into it. Some less than pleasant things have happened since the death of dear Mother. Perhaps the time will come for them, too, and perhaps it will come sooner than we expect. I'm missing things in the business, perhaps it's not that things are being done behind my back—I'm not at all saying that they're being done behind my back—I don't have the strength any more, my memory's going, I can't keep my eye on all the moving parts like I used to. That's partly nature taking its course, first of all, and secondly the death of darling Mother perhaps hit me harder than it did you. But since we're talking about this now, about this letter, I ask you, Georg, don't lie to me. This is such a trivial question, hardly worth speaking about, so don't lie to me. Do you really have this friend in St Petersburg?"

Georg stood up in embarrassment. "Let's leave my friends for now. A thousand friends wouldn't be enough to replace my father. You know what I think? You're not taking care of yourself enough. And age takes a toll. You're indispensable to me at work, but if the business ever put your health at risk, I'd close it down tomorrow. That goes without saying. We've got to start you on a different way of life. From the ground up. You're sitting here in the dark, and in the living room it's nice and bright. You're picking at your breakfast instead of keeping up your strength. You're sitting here with the window shut when the fresh air would do you so much good. No, Father! I'm going to fetch the doctor and we're going to do what he prescribes. We're going to swap rooms: you can move into the front room, I'll move in here. You won't have to change anything, we'll move all your things across with you. But there's plenty of time for all that, just have a lie down for the time being, I'm sure you need some rest. Here, I'll help you get undressed, you'll see that I can do it. Or if you want to move into the front room right away, you can just get into my bed. That would be very sensible."

Georg was standing close in front of his father, who had let his head with its messy white hair sink to his chest.

"Georg," his father said quietly, without moving.

Georg immediately knelt in front of his father. In his tired face he saw overlarge pupils in half-shut eyes, looking at him.

"You don't have a friend in St Petersburg. You've always been a practical joker and you haven't held back even with me. How *could* you have a friend there, of all places? You can't expect me to believe that."

"Just think back, Father," said Georg, helping his father out of his chair and taking his dressing gown off him while he stood there, really quite weak on his feet. "It was nearly three years ago, my friend was here visiting us. I remember that you didn't like him very much. I ended up disowning him to you, it happened at least twice, even though he was sitting right there in my room. I thought that disliking him was completely understandable; after all, my friend can be quite odd. But then after that you finally had a very good chat with him. I remember being proud that you were listening to him, nodding your head and asking him questions. If you think back, you'll be sure to remember. He was telling us these unbelievable stories about the Russian Revolution. About how once when he was on a business trip to Kiev he got caught up in some pandemonium and saw a priest on a balcony cut a bloody cross into the palm of his hand, hold it up and shout to the mob. I've even heard you tell that story yourself from time to time."

Meanwhile Georg had managed to sit his father down again and carefully take off the pyjama trousers he wore over his linen underwear, as well as his socks. At the sight of the not particularly clean underwear, Georg began to reproach himself for neglecting his father. There was no doubt it was his responsibility to oversee the regular changing of his father's underwear. How to arrange his father's future was something he and his fiancée hadn't yet explicitly discussed, because they'd tacitly assumed that his father would stay on alone in the old apartment. But now he quickly and firmly decided that he would take his father with him into his new household. On closer inspection, it almost seemed as if the care Georg would then arrange might already be too late.

He carried his father to bed. A horrible sensation came over him when he realized, as he took the few paces across the room, that his father was playing with the watch chain hanging from Georg's chest. He held on to it so tightly that at first Georg couldn't put him down.

But as soon as he was in bed everything seemed fine. He got under the covers himself and then pulled the blanket up past his shoulders. He looked up at Georg with a not unfriendly expression.

"Isn't that right, you're already starting to remember him?" asked Georg, nodding at him encouragingly.

"Am I properly covered up?" asked his father, as if he couldn't check whether his feet were sticking out.

"So you're very happy in bed," said Georg, and rearranged the blanket into a better position.

"Am I properly covered up?" his father asked again, seeming to pay especially close attention to the answer.

"Just rest easy, you're properly covered up."

"No!" his father shouted almost before Georg had finished speaking, threw back the blanket with such force that it unfurled itself in mid-air, and stood upright on the bed. He lightly held on to the ceiling with one hand. "You wanted to cover me up, I know that, sunshine, but I'm not buried yet. And even if this is the last of my strength, it's enough for you, too much for you. Of course I know your friend. He would have been a son after my own heart. That's why you've strung him along all these years. Why else? Do you really think I never wept for him? That's why you lock yourself in your office, you're not to be disturbed, the boss is busy—just so you can send your lying little letters to Russia. But luckily no one needs to teach a father how to see through his son. Now that you think you've done him down, done him so far down you can sit your arse on him and he won't even move, my little lord of a son has decided he will marry!"

Georg gazed up at this terrible vision of his father. The fate of his friend in St Petersburg, whom his father suddenly knew so well, struck him as never before. He saw him lost in the Russian expanses. He saw him at the door of his empty, looted shop. Among the wreckage of the shelves, the shredded goods, the broken gas fittings, he was only just still standing. Why did he have to move so far away!

"But look at me!" cried his father, and Georg, almost losing his mind, ran over to the bed to grab on to something, but faltered halfway there.

"Because she lifted up her skirt," his father began to warble, "because she lifted up her skirt like this, that horrible tramp." And to demonstrate what he meant, he lifted his nightshirt so high that you could see the scar from his war years on his thigh. "Because she lifted up her skirt like this and this and this, you threw yourself at her, and so that you can gratify yourself without any interruptions, you've disgraced Mother's memory, betrayed your friend and tried to stick your father in bed so he can't move a muscle. But can he still move or can't he?"

He stood totally unsupported and kicked his legs. He beamed with insight.

Georg stood in a corner, as far as possible from his father. A long time ago he'd resolved to observe everything that happened completely and precisely, so that he couldn't be taken by surprise if something came at him from behind or dropped on him from above. Now he remembered that long-forgotten resolution and promptly forgot it again, just as you can unwittingly pull a short thread out of the eye of a needle.

"But your friend hasn't been betrayed!" his father cried, waving a finger back and forth to reinforce what he was saying. "I've been his representative here on the ground."

"Clown!" Georg couldn't stop himself from shouting; he recognized the damage at once and, too late, his eyes fixed, bit into his tongue so hard he flinched in pain.

"Yes, I've been clowning! Clowning! Good word! What other consolation is there for a widowed old father? Well—and for the moment let's say you're still my living son—what else is left for me, in my back room, hounded by disloyal staff, old to the marrow? While my son merrily swans around, closing deals that I prepared, falling over himself with smugness, and parading about in front of his own father with the reserved expression of an honourable gentleman! Do you think I didn't love you—I, the one you came from?"

'Now he'll bend forward,' thought Georg, 'if only he'd fall and shatter into pieces!' This phrase whistled through his head.

His father bent forward, but didn't fall. Since Georg didn't come closer, as he'd expected he would, he lifted himself up again.

"Stay where you are, I don't need you! You think you've still got the strength to come over to me and that you're just holding yourself back because that's what you choose to do. How wrong you are! I'm still the stronger of us by far. If I'd been on my own I might have had to give way, but Mother passed on her strength to me, I've made a lovely alliance with your friend, I've got your clients here in my pocket!"

'Even in his shroud he's got pockets!' Georg said to himself, and thought that this observation would make it impossible for his father to exist. Only for an instant did he hold that thought, then as always he forgot it entirely.

"Just try coming to see me with your fiancée on your arm! I'll swat her aside like you can hardly imagine!"

Georg frowned as if doubting that were true. His father just nodded towards Georg's corner, asserting what he'd said.

"I found it so funny today when you came to ask whether you should write to your friend about your engagement! He already knows everything, you stupid boy, he knows everything! I've been writing to him, because you forgot to take my writing things away. That's why he hasn't come for years, he knows everything a hundred times better than you do yourself, he scrunches up your letters unread in his left hand while he holds up mine in his right!"

He swung his arm over his head in enthusiasm. "He knows everything a thousand times better!"

"Ten thousand times!" said Georg, to deride his father, but as he said the words, they came out sounding deadly earnest.

"For years I've been waiting for you to come to me with this question! Do you think I care about anything else? Do you think I read the paper? There!" And he tossed Georg a page from a newspaper that had somehow been carried with him into bed. An old paper with a name that Georg didn't even recognize.

"How long you hesitated before you were finally ready! Your mother had to die, she didn't live to see the happy day, your friend has been falling apart out there in Russia, even three years ago he was so sick it was all but over, and me, well, you can see what condition I'm in. You've still got eyes for that!"

"You ambushed me!" shouted Georg.

His father said pityingly: "You probably wanted to say that earlier. Now it doesn't make sense any more."

And louder: "So now you know what else there is besides you; before now you only knew about yourself! You were an innocent child, really, but as a man you've been a fiend! — So pay attention: I now sentence you to death by drowning!"

Georg felt chased out of the room, with the crash of his father falling onto the bed ringing in his ears. On the stairs, which he rushed down as if they were a smooth slope, he bowled into his cleaning woman, who was just going up to tidy the apartment for the morning. She shouted "Jesus!" and covered her face with her apron, but he was already gone. He burst out of the door and raced across the road towards the water. A moment later, he was gripping the railing like a starving man grips food. He swung himself over it like the excellent gymnast he'd been in his teenage years, to the pride of his parents. He clung on, his hands weakening, until between the railing's posts he saw a bus approaching that would easily cover the noise of his fall, then cried out softly, "Dear parents, haven't I always loved you?" and let himself drop.

Meanwhile an almost endless stream of traffic went over the bridge.

THE TRUTH ABOUT
SANCHO PANZA

S ANCHO PANZA—who incidentally has never boasted about this—used to leave out piles of novels about knights and robbers in the evenings and for the long hours of the night, and by doing so for several years he succeeded in distracting his devil, whom he later gave the name Don Quixote, so completely that this devil threw himself into all kinds of crazy exploits, which, because they lacked a definite target—it should have been Sancho Panza—never hurt anyone. Sancho Panza, a free man, calmly followed Don Quixote on his quests, perhaps out of a sense of responsibility, and got a great deal of edifying entertainment from him till the end of his days.

THE BRIDGE

I WAS STIFF AND COLD, I was a bridge, I lay across a ravine. My feet were dug into one cliff, my hands into the other, I gripped the crumbling clay. The tails of my coat fluttered at my sides. Deep below me roared an icy trout river. No tourist ever strayed up to these trackless heights, the bridge wasn't even marked on the maps. — So I lay there and waited; there was nothing else I could do. Unless it collapses, a bridge once built can never stop being a bridge.

One day, it was towards evening—was it the first evening, was it the thousandth? I can't say, my thoughts were confused, going round in circles. Towards evening, in the summer, when the rushing water was getting darker, I heard the footsteps of a man. Coming to me, to me. — Stretch out your span, I said to myself; get your planks ready; carry the one who's been entrusted to you. If his steps are uncertain, steady them without his noticing; but if he stumbles, reveal yourself and, like a mountain god, hurl him to the ground.

He came, he tapped me with his walking stick's iron tip, he lifted up my coat-tails with it and arranged them on me. He stuck the tip into my unruly hair and left it there for a long time, no doubt while he gazed wildly around him. But then—as I lay above the mountains and the ravine, dreaming of him—he jumped with both feet onto the middle of my body. I shuddered in bewildered pain, not understanding. Who was he? A child? A dream? A robber? A suicide? A tempter? A destroyer? And I turned around to look at him. — A bridge turning around! I hadn't even finished turning when I started to fall, I fell, and already I was being torn and impaled by the sharp rocks that had always stared up at me so peacefully from the raging waters.

THE MARRIED COUPLE

B USINESS IS SO BAD at the moment that sometimes, if I'm just killing time in the office, I take the sample case and go see the clients myself. I'd also been meaning to go and pay a visit to N. for a while, because we used to work together all the time and in the past year, I don't know why, it's faded almost to nothing. Changes like that actually don't have to happen for a reason; in today's unstable conditions, a nothing, a mood, can make the difference, and in the same way a nothing, a few words, can get everything back on track. But it is a bit tricky going to see N.; he's an old man, he's been very sick recently, and even though he's still in control of all his affairs, he hardly ever goes into the office any more; if you want to speak to him, you have to go to his apartment, and that's the kind of business trip you're happy to keep postponing.

Anyway, yesterday evening at six I set off for where he lives; it was certainly past the usual time for going to see someone, but it needed to be looked at from a business angle, not as a social visit. N. was at home; they told me in the front room that he'd just come back in from a walk with his wife and gone in to see his son, who wasn't well and was lying in bed. I was told to go through; I hesitated at first, but then that feeling was overruled by the desire to get this painful visit over as quickly as possible, and so, still in my hat and coat and carrying my sample case, I let myself be led through a dark corridor into a dimly lit room where a small group had gathered.

I suppose out of instinct, the first thing I noticed was a sales rep I know all too well and who is also partly a competitor. He'd sneaked his way up here even before I had. He'd found a comfortable spot right beside the invalid's bed, as if he were the doctor; in his lovely, fluffed-up, open jacket, he sat in his chair like he was in charge of the room; I've never met anyone so brazen; I thought the invalid might be thinking something similar as he lay there with fever-flushed cheeks and occasionally glanced up at him. Incidentally, he's not young any more, the son, he's a man my age with a short beard that's become a little unkempt in his illness. Old man N. is big and broad-shouldered, and I was shocked to see that his slow suffering had made him gaunt, bent and uncertain. He was standing there just as he'd come in, still in his furs, and mumbling something at his son. His wife, small and fragile, albeit very animated, even if only towards him—she never looked at the rest of us—was busy helping him out of the furs, which was difficult because of the height difference between them, but she finally managed it. Perhaps the real difficulty was that N. was very impatient and kept reaching out his hands to demand the armchair, which his wife quickly pushed across to him once the furs were off. She took the furs away herself, even though she almost disappeared under them, and carried them out of the room.

Now it seemed that my moment had come, or rather, it hadn't come and was probably never going to come; but if I was going to attempt something, I had to do it right away because I had the feeling that the circumstances were only going to get even less conducive to a business conversation; settling in here until the end of time, which seemed to be the sales rep's plan, was not my style; and it wasn't as if I was going to hold back on his account. So without much ado I started to present my thinking, even though I noticed that N. wanted to speak to his son. Unfortunately, I've got this bad habit that, if I work myself up with talk—something that can happen very quickly and that happened even faster than usual in that sickroom—I stand up and start pacing up and down while I speak. It's no bad thing when you're in your own office, but in a stranger's home it really is a bit much. I couldn't get myself under control, especially because I didn't have my usual cigarette to hand. Now, everyone's got their bad habits, and I would say that at least mine aren't as bad as the sales rep's. What can you say about someone who, for example, slides his hat slowly back and forth across his knees, but then suddenly, for no reason, puts it on his head; he'd take it off again right away, as if there was some mistake, but then a moment later he had it on his head again, and he kept repeating this routine, on and off. A performance like that you have to say is unacceptable. But in this moment, it doesn't bother me, I pace up and down, completely caught up in my affairs, and ignore him; some people might have been thrown entirely off their stride by that hat business. Anyway, in my eagerness I don't pay any attention to these distractions; in fact, I don't pay any to anyone; of course I can see what's happening but, so long as I'm not finished and not hearing any objections, I somehow don't register it. So for example, I noticed that N. wasn't very receptive to what I was saying; he had his hands on the armrests and was shifting awkwardly from side to side, not looking at me, but staring blankly into space, and his expression was as indifferent as if not a single word I was saying, nor even the fact that I was there, was getting through to him. I did see this distracted behaviour, which was far from encouraging, but I carried on talking regardless, as if there were some chance that the very advantageous offers I was presenting—I shocked myself with the concessions I made, concessions no one had asked for—as if this might bring everything back onto an even keel. It also gave me a certain satisfaction to see that the rep, as I noticed in passing, had finally left his hat alone and crossed his arms in front of his chest; my presentation, which was naturally also aimed at him, seemed to have put a big hole in his plans. And with the sense of well-being I got from that, I might have gone on talking even longer if the son, who until then I'd disregarded as irrelevant, abruptly lifted himself up in bed and shook his fist at me until I stopped. He apparently wanted to say something, or show us something, but didn't have the strength. At first I thought he was just a bit delirious, but when I inadvertently glanced across at old N., I started to understand.

His eyes were open, glassy, bulging and only just still working, while he himself was shaking and leaning forward as if someone was pushing or hitting him in the back of the neck; his lower lip, his whole lower jaw, was hanging down loose away from his gums, his entire face seemed to be coming apart; he was still breathing, albeit heavily, but then he fell back into the chair as if liberated, closed his eyes, the expression of some great effort crossed his face at the last, and then he was gone. I quickly leapt over to him and took his cold, lifeless, shudder-inducing hand; there was no pulse. So, it was all over. An old man. May our own deaths come as easily. But there was so much that had to be done right now! And in this haste, what to do first? I looked around for help; but the son had pulled the covers over his head and you could hear his endless sobbing; the sales rep, cold as a frog, sat there in his chair, two steps from N., visibly determined to do nothing and wait for time to pass; so there was only me who might do something, and the thing to do was the hardest thing of all, namely to give his wife the news in some way she could take, that is, in some way that didn't exist anywhere on earth.

She brought in—she was still in her street clothes; she hadn't yet had time to change—she brought in a nightshirt that had been warmed on the oven and that she wanted her husband to put on. "He's fallen asleep," she said, smiling and shaking her head, when she found us in this tableau. And with the boundless trust of the innocent, she picked up the same hand that I'd just touched with revulsion and shame, kissed it with marital playfulness and—while the three of us stared—N. shifted, yawned, let her put the nightshirt on him, tolerated with ironic annoyance her tender criticisms about having overexerted himself on the long walk, and, strangely enough, in order to give a different reason for having fallen asleep, said something about being bored. Then, so as not to catch a chill going through into the other room, he lay down for a moment in the bed next to his son; his head was bedded down next to his son's feet on a couple of cushions his wife quickly brought over. After what had just happened, I didn't think there was anything odd about it. Then he asked for the evening paper, took it despite the presence of his guests, but didn't yet start reading, just glanced across the pages and told us, with astonishing acumen, some deeply uncomfortable truths about the offers we'd made, all the while making a gesture with his hand as if throwing us away and clicking his tongue to show us what a bad taste our behaviour had left in his mouth. The sales rep couldn't stop himself from making a few poorly judged remarks; even his dull senses seemed to feel that, after what had just happened, things had to be brought back on track in some way, but with his crude manners that was never going to work. I said my goodbyes quickly; I was almost grateful to the rep for being there; without him I might not have had the decisiveness to leave so fast.

In the hallway I met Frau N. Seeing the downtrodden figure she cut, I said straight out that she reminded me a little of my mother. And when she didn't respond, I added, "Whatever you might say about it, she could work miracles. Things that we'd destroyed, she made whole again. I lost her when I was still a child." I'd intentionally spoken very slowly and clearly because I suspected the old woman was hard of hearing. But she must have been all but deaf, because she asked me in reply, "And how does my husband look to you?" From the few words we exchanged as I left, I also realized that she had me mixed up with the sales rep; I wanted to believe that she would otherwise have been a bit more forthcoming.

Then I went down the stairs. The way down was harder than the way up had been, and that hadn't been easy either. Oh, what futile paths we're compelled to tread as we go about our business, and how much further we have to carry our burdens.

BEFORE THE LAW

BEFORE THE LAW there's a gatekeeper. A man from the country comes up to this gatekeeper and asks to be admitted to the law. But the gatekeeper says that he can't let him in right now. The man thinks it over and then asks whether he'll be allowed to go in later. "It's possible," says the gatekeeper, "but not at the moment." Since the door to the law is open, as always, and since the gatekeeper has stepped to the side, the man bends forward to look through the entrance and see what's in there. When the gatekeeper notices, he laughs and says, "If you're that desperate, you could try going in even though I've told you not to. But bear in mind: I'm very strong. And I'm only the lowest-ranking gatekeeper. From room to room there are more gatekeepers, each stronger than the last. Just the sight of the third one is more than I can take." The man from the country hadn't expected so much difficulty; after all, the law should be available to anyone at any time, he thinks, but as he takes a closer look at the gatekeeper in his fur-lined coat, at his big, pointed

46

nose, his long, thin, black Tartar-like beard, he decides
that he'd actually rather wait until he gets permission to
go in. The gatekeeper gives him a stool and has him sit
down to one side of the door. He sits there for days and
years. He makes many attempts to be let in and tires out
the gatekeeper with his pleas. The gatekeeper sometimes
cross-examines him a little, asking him about where he
comes from and many other things besides, but they're
detached questions, of the kind very grand people ask,
and in the end he always says that he can't let the man
in yet. The man, who'd outfitted himself with all sorts of
things for the journey, uses everything he has, no matter
how valuable, to try and bribe the gatekeeper. The gatekeeper accepts it all, but says, "I'm just taking this so you
don't think there's something you haven't tried." Over
the course of these many years, the man watches the
gatekeeper almost uninterruptedly. He forgets the other
gatekeepers and begins to believe that this one is the only
obstacle between him and the law. He curses his bad luck,
loudly and recklessly for the first few years, then, later,
when he gets old, he just grumbles under his breath. He
becomes childish and, since he has studied the gatekeeper
so long he's familiar even with the fleas in his fur collar, he
begs the fleas to help him change the gatekeeper's mind.
Finally, the light in his eyes grows weak and he doesn't
know whether it's really getting dark or just that his eyes
are tricking him. But in this darkness he can't miss the

splendour that pours inextinguishably out of the door to the law. He doesn't live much longer. Before he dies, all his experiences from these many years gather in his head to form a question that he'd never asked the gatekeeper before. He waves him closer because he can no longer lift his stiffening body. The gatekeeper has to lean right down to him, since the size difference between them has grown much larger. "What is it you want to know now?" asks the gatekeeper. "You're insatiable."

"Everybody wants the law," says the man, "so why is it that in all this time no one apart from me has asked to be let in?"

The gatekeeper can see that the man is near the end and, to get through to his failing hearing, he shouts at the top of his voice: "No one else could come in this way because this entrance was reserved only for you. I'll go now and close it."

A HUNGER ARTIST

I N THE PAST FEW DECADES public interest in the art of fasting has drastically declined. While it used to be very profitable to put on big, stand-alone exhibitions, doing so today would be completely impossible. It was another time. Back then, the whole city would get caught up in what the hunger artist was doing; the audience would grow and grow as the fast went on; everyone wanted to see him at least once a day; in the latter stages, you'd get fans who wanted to sit in front of the small cage from dawn till dusk; there were also viewings at night, with the effect heightened by flaming torches; on sunny days, the cage would be carried outside and children would be brought to see the hunger artist; whereas for adults he was often only a bit of fun, whom they went to see because it was fashionable, the children gazed at him in amazement, their mouths open, holding each other's hands just in case something happened, while he, disdaining even a chair, sat on a scattering of straw, pale, in a black vest through which you could see his ribs sticking out, sometimes nodding politely, sometimes answering questions with an effortful smile, even stretching his arm out through the bars to let them feel how emaciated he was, then sinking back into himself, paying attention to nothing, not even the clock, which was the only furniture in his cage and struck the hours that were so important to him, but only staring into space with his eyes almost shut, and now and then sipping water from a tiny glass just to keep his lips wet.

As well as the spectators, who came and went, there were also warders chosen by the public—strangely enough, they were usually butchers—whose job it was to watch the hunger artist day and night, always three at a time, so that he couldn't secretly take a bite of food. But it was only a formality introduced to reassure the audiences, because those involved knew full well that during a fast the artist would never, under no circumstances, not even under duress, have eaten even the tiniest snack; the honour of his art forbade it. It's true that not every warder could understand that; you sometimes got groups of warders who'd do a very lax job of watching the artist at night, intentionally sitting together in a remote corner of the room and engrossing themselves in a game of cards with the obvious intention of allowing the artist to gulp some small morsel that they imagined he'd be able to produce from somewhere. Nothing was more painful to the hunger artist than this kind of warder; they lowered his spirits; they made the hunger incredibly hard to bear; sometimes he gathered enough strength to sing during these watches, for as long as he could, to show these people how wrong they were to be suspicious of him. But it hardly helped; they just wondered about how he'd learnt to sing and eat at the same time. He much preferred the warders who sat up close against the bars, who weren't satisfied by the dim lighting in the hall and fixed him with electric torches that the impresario provided. The harsh light didn't bother him at all, he couldn't fall properly asleep anyway, and he could always doze a little, regardless of how bright or what time it was, even when the hall was packed and noisy. With warders like these he was very willing to pass the night without any sleep; he was ready to joke around with them, to tell them stories from his nomadic life or to listen to their stories, anything to keep them awake and show them over and over again that there was nothing edible in his cage and that he was fasting as none of them ever could have. But he was at his happiest when morning came and they were brought an enormous breakfast, billed to him, which they threw themselves on with the appetite of healthy men who'd spent a long night at their posts. A few people managed to convince themselves that these breakfasts were an attempt to unduly influence the warders, but that really was going too far, and when they were asked whether they'd like to prove the point by taking the night watch themselves, without any breakfast, they made themselves scarce, albeit without giving up their scepticism.

These, however, were merely some of the suspicions that were inseparable from the art of fasting. After all, no single person could spend every day and night uninterruptedly watching the artist, so no one could tell with his own eyes whether the artist really was fasting uninterruptedly, that is, flawlessly; only the hunger artist was in a position to know that; he himself was the only spectator who could have been completely satisfied by his fast. But there were other considerations that meant satisfaction always eluded him. In fact, it was perhaps not even the fasting itself that emaciated him so much that some people had to stay away from the performances, to their regret, because they couldn't bear to look at him; perhaps he was only so emaciated because of his dissatisfaction with himself. He alone knew something that even the most obsessive fans didn't, namely how easy it was to fast. It was the easiest thing in the world. He didn't try to hide it, but no one believed him; at best they thought him modest, but usually they assumed that he was looking for publicity or even that he was a cheat who found fasting easy because he'd found some means of making it easy, and now even had the chutzpah to more or less admit it. He had to put up with all this, had got used to it over the years, but on the inside this dissatisfaction was always gnawing at him and he had never, in no fast—he insisted on having a certificate stating this made out—he had never willingly left the cage. The maximum fasting time had been set by the impresario at forty days; he never let it go on beyond that, not even in the capital cities, and for good reason. Experience showed that, for about forty days, ever increasing publicity could whip up a city's interest to greater and greater heights, but after that the audiences would start to dwindle and there would be a marked tailing off in the show's popularity; of course there might be small differences between cities and countries, but as a rule it was true that forty days was the maximum. So on the fortieth day the door to the flower-bedecked cage was opened, a rapturous audience packed the amphitheatre, a brass band played, two doctors went into the cage to perform the necessary tests on the hunger artist, the results were relayed to the spectators through a megaphone, and last of all came two young ladies, who were very happy to have won the raffle and now wanted to lead the hunger artist out of the cage and down a couple of steps to a little table where a carefully prepared recovery meal had been laid out. And in that moment the hunger artist always resisted. Although he would willingly put his bony arms into the helpfully outstretched hands of the two ladies bending down to him, he didn't want to get up. Why stop now after forty days of hunger? He could have held out much longer, indefinitely; why stop when he was at the peak, not even yet at the peak, of his fast? Why did they want to deny him the fame of fasting longer, of becoming not just the greatest hunger artist of all time, which he probably already was, but also of surpassing himself and carrying on into a performance that was beyond human understanding—because he could feel no limits to his capacity for hunger. Why did these crowds, who claimed to admire him so much, have so little patience with him; if he could hold out for longer, why shouldn't they? Also he was tired and sitting comfortably on the straw, and they wanted him to get up and walk over to this meal, the mere thought of which made him feel nauseous, something he only suppressed, with difficulty, out of consideration for the ladies. And he looked up into the eyes of the ladies who seemed so friendly but were in reality so cruel, and shook his over-heavy head on his weak neck. But then happened what always happened. The impresario came and silently—the music made talking impossible—raised his arms above the hunger artist, as if inviting the heavens to look at his work here on the straw, this pitiable martyr, something the hunger artist certainly was, albeit in a quite different sense; he clasped the hunger artist around his thin waist, taking exaggerated care to show everyone what a fragile object he was handling, and—subtly shaking him a little so that the hunger artist's legs and upper body swayed loosely back and forth—handed him over to the young ladies, who were now deathly pale. After that, the hunger artist

acquiesced to everything; his head lay on his chest as if it
had rolled there and inexplicably stopped; his torso had
been hollowed out; his legs pressed themselves together
at the knees as if in self-preservation, dragging along the
ground as though it wasn't real and the real ground was
somewhere below it; and the whole, very small, weight of
his body was deposited on one of the young ladies, who,
appealing for help and hyperventilating—this was not how
she'd imagined her honorary task—at first stretched out
her neck as far as possible to keep at least her face from
touching the hunger artist, then, when that didn't work
and her luckier companion didn't help, made do with
reaching out, trembling, to the artist's hand and carrying that little packet of bones ahead of herself, the first
young lady burst into tears, to the delighted laughter of
the amphitheatre, and had to be relieved by an attendant
who'd long been standing by for that very purpose. Then
came the meal, a few scraps of which the impresario
pushed into the hunger artist, who was in a half-sleep
bordering on unconsciousness, while the impresario kept
up an entertaining patter that was intended to distract
attention from the state the artist was in; finally a toast
was drunk to the audience, supposedly at the whispered
suggestion of the artist; the band confirmed everything
with a mighty flourish, people went their separate ways,
and nobody had any right to be dissatisfied with what he'd
seen, nobody, only the hunger artist, always only him.

With regular short rest periods, he was able to live this way for many years, in apparent glory, feted by the world, but nevertheless usually in a gloomy mood that became steadily gloomier because nobody would take it seriously. After all, what could they have comforted him with? What more could he wish for? And if occasionally he met some good-natured person who sympathized and tried to explain that his sadness was probably a consequence of hunger, it sometimes happened, especially if he was deep into a fasting period, that the hunger artist would react with a fit of rage, frightening the audience by rattling at his cage like an animal. But the impresario had a punishment he liked to employ for these outbursts. He apologized to the assembled public on the artist's behalf and admitted that nothing could excuse his behaviour except the irritability caused by hunger, something well-fed people could hardly understand; then he came on to the claims made by the hunger artist—which, after all, also needed an explanation—that he would be able to fast for far longer than he did; the impresario praised the noble endeavour, the goodwill, the great self-denial that was certainly bound up in that claim; but then he refuted it simply enough, by showing photographs—which were also on sale—of the artist on his fortieth fast day, in bed, so enfeebled he was almost extinguished. This twisting of the facts, which was well known to the hunger artist but always unnerved him all over again, was too much for him. The consequences of prematurely ending the fast were being presented as the reason for doing so! Against that unreason, to fight against this world of unreason, was impossible. Every time this came up he would listen greedily at the bars, in good faith, but when the photographs appeared he would let go of the bars, sink back into the straw with a sigh, and the reassured spectators could come and view him again.

When the people who witnessed these scenes thought back a couple of years later, they often found that they no longer understood what they'd been doing there. Because by then the collapse in public interest mentioned above had taken place; it happened suddenly; there may have been deeper reasons for it, but who cared enough to dig around for them; in any case, one day the pampered hunger artist found that the pleasure-seeking crowds had abandoned him and now preferred to go to other kinds of performance. Once again the impresario rushed him through half of Europe, to see whether here and there they might still find a flicker of the old interest; all in vain; as if in some secret pact, audiences everywhere had developed a downright aversion to performance fasting. Of course things like that couldn't change overnight, and in retrospect they remembered several warning signs that had been insufficiently heeded or addressed amid the intoxication of fame, but it was too late to do anything about it now. Although it was certain that the art of fasting's time would one day come again, that was no comfort to those living through this moment. What was the hunger artist supposed to do? He, who'd been celebrated by thousands, couldn't start displaying himself in a booth at local fairs, and as for taking up another profession, the artist was not only too old, he was above all too fanatically devoted to his hunger. So he said goodbye to the impresario, who'd been his companion in an unparalleled career, and had himself taken on by a travelling circus; to spare his own feelings, he didn't even look at the terms of the contract.

A big circus with its myriad of people and animals and apparatuses, all complementing and offsetting one another, can find a use for anybody at any time, even a hunger artist, on appropriately modest terms of course, and moreover in this particular case it was not just the hunger artist himself who'd been hired, but also his famous old name; given the unique nature of this art form, which made no concessions to advancing age, you couldn't have said that a veteran artist past his prime was retreating into a quiet circus job; on the contrary, the hunger artist assured them that he would fast just as well as he ever had, which was entirely credible, and went so far as to claim that, if he was allowed to have his way— something that was promised out of hand—he would astonish the world as he'd never been able to before, a claim that, in view of the fashions of the day, which the hunger artist forgot in his enthusiasm, elicited no more than a smile from the experts.

Overall, however, even the hunger artist didn't lose sight of the real state of affairs and took it as read that his cage wouldn't be placed in the centre of the ring as a star attraction, but was found a home outside, in an actually very easily accessible spot just next to the menagerie. Big, colourfully painted signs framed the cage and announced what could be seen inside. In the intervals in the main show, when the audience streamed out to see the animals, it was almost inevitable that they passed by the hunger artist and paused there for a moment. They might have stayed there longer had it not been that the passage was narrow and that those pushing on from the back of the crowd, who didn't understand this delay on the way to the eagerly anticipated menagerie, made any slower, quieter viewing impossible. That was why the viewing times, which he naturally looked forward to since they were the purpose of his life, also made him tremble. At first he could hardly wait for the intervals in the main show; he'd been exhilarated as he prepared to face the onrushing masses, but all too soon—even his most obstinate, almost conscious self-deception couldn't withstand what he experienced—he became convinced that if you categorized these spectators by what they wanted to see, they were all, always and without exception, visitors to the menagerie. The first sight of them, from a distance, remained the most pleasant. When they had got up close, he was surrounded by a racket of shouting and swearing between the two groups that always formed, those—who soon became almost more painful to the hunger artist—who wanted to have a good look at him, not out of understanding, but on a whim or out of spite; and those who truly only wanted to get to the menagerie. Once the main bulk of them had gone by, there were always a few stragglers, who had nothing to prevent them stopping as long as they liked, but they hurried past with long strides, barely glancing sideways, to make sure they saw the animals in time. All too rarely did a father come past with his children, point his finger at the artist, explain what was going on, tell them how it had been years ago, when he'd gone to similar but incomparably grander performances; the children hadn't been prepared by school or life to really understand—after all, what was fasting to them?—but in their bright, curious eyes he saw a sign of new, more favourable, times to come. Perhaps, the hunger artist then sometimes said to himself, it would be better after all if he wasn't positioned so near the menagerie. His being there made the choice between him and the animals too easy for people, not to mention that the smell of the stalls, the animals' restlessness at night, the slabs of raw meat being brought to the carnivores and the uproar at feeding time all upset and depressed him. But he didn't dare take a grievance to the management; at the end of the day, he owed the animals the crowds of visitors who trooped past him and among whom one or two of the right sort might appear; and who knew where the management would stick him if he reminded them that he existed and that, strictly speaking, he was an obstacle on the way to the menagerie.

A small obstacle though, an ever smaller obstacle. People grew used to the strangeness of a circus trying to attract attention with a hunger artist in this day and age, and with that his fate was sealed. He was free to fast as hard as he could, and did so, but nothing now could save him, and the public simply walked past. Try explaining the art of hunger! If someone doesn't feel it, you can't make them understand. The lovely signs on his cage grew dirty and illegible; they were torn down and no one thought to replace them; the little board displaying the number of days he'd fasted—which at first had been diligently updated every morning—had now long remained unchanged, because after a few weeks the attendants grew bored of even that small job; and so although the hunger artist fasted just as he'd dreamt of doing, and although he effortlessly succeeded in holding out ever longer, just as he'd predicted, no one counted the days, no one, not even the hunger artist himself, knew exactly how much he'd achieved, and his heart grew heavy. Now when someone idling by happened to stop, to make fun of the number on the board and talk about it being a con, it was tantamount to the stupidest lie that indifference and malice could have concocted, because the hunger artist didn't cheat, he did his work honestly, but the world cheated him of his reward.

But many days again went by and this, too, came to an end. A supervisor noticed the cage and asked the attendants why this useful piece of equipment had been left standing around with nothing but some rotten straw inside it; no one could say, until someone looked at the board with the numbers and remembered the hunger artist. They poked through the straw with poles and found the artist underneath. "You're still fasting?" asked the supervisor. "When are you finally going to stop?"

"Forgive me, all of you," whispered the hunger artist; only the supervisor, whose ear was to the bars, could hear him.

"Of course," said the supervisor, putting a finger to his temple to show his staff what condition the artist was in. "We forgive you."

"I always wanted you to admire my fasting," said the hunger artist.

"And we do admire it," the supervisor said obligingly.

"But you shouldn't admire it," said the hunger artist.

"All right, then we don't admire it," said the supervisor, "but why shouldn't we admire it?"

"Because I have to fast, I can't help it," said the hunger artist.

"How about that," said the supervisor. "So why can't you help it?"

"Because," said the hunger artist, and he lifted his head a little, pursing his lips as if for a kiss, so he could speak right into the supervisor's ear and make sure nothing was lost, "I couldn't find a meal I would have liked to eat. If I'd found one, believe me, I wouldn't have made a fuss, I'd have eaten till I was full, just like you or anyone else." Those were his last words, but in his broken eyes there remained the firm, albeit no longer proud, conviction that he would go on fasting.

"Get this cleared up!" said the supervisor, and they buried the hunger artist together with the straw. In the cage they put a young panther. Even the most stolid attendants felt the relief of seeing this wild animal throwing himself around the long-deserted cage. He lacked for nothing. The keepers brought him the food he liked as a matter of course; he didn't even seem to miss his freedom; his glorious body, endowed almost to bursting with all it needed, seemed to carry its own freedom within itself; it seemed to lurk somewhere in the panther's jaws; and the joy of life steamed out of his mouth with such force that the spectators felt they could barely hold their ground against it. But they braced themselves, crowded around the cage and never wanted to leave.

THE TREES

W<small>E'RE LIKE TREE TRUNKS</small> in the snow. They seem to stand on its surface, as if a little push would be enough to knock them over. No, you can't do that, because they're fixed firmly to the ground. But look, even that is illusory.

THE NEW LAWYER

W E'VE GOT A NEW LAWYER, a Dr Bucephalus. There's not much in his appearance to remind you that he used to be Alexander of Macedon's war horse. But if you know his background, there are a few things you notice. That said, I did recently see even a pretty simple-minded court usher admiring our lawyer with the practised eye of a regular racegoer as he bounded up the stairs, lifting his knees high and letting his steps ring out on the marble.

In general, the office approves of Bucephalus having been taken on. With a surprising degree of sympathy, people say that the way society is arranged today puts Bucephalus in a difficult position and for that reason, as well as on account of his historical significance, we should be as accommodating as possible. Nowadays—this is something no one can deny—there is no Alexander the Great. It's true that some people still know about killing; nor is the skill needed to spear a friend across the banqueting table wholly a lost art; there are plenty of people who find Macedonia too small and curse Philip, his father—but there is no one, no one, capable of leading us to India. Even in those days, the gates of India seemed unreachable, but the direction was given by the king's sword. Today the gates are altogether elsewhere, higher and further off; no one is pointing the way; it's true that lots of people have swords, but only to wave them about, and anyone who tries to follow them with his eyes ends up bewildered.

That's why it's maybe best to do what Bucephalus has and bury yourself in the law books. Free, his sides no longer being gripped by his rider's thighs, under restful lamplight far from the clamour of Alexander's battles, he reads and turns the pages of our dusty old books.

AN OLD JOURNAL

I T SOMETIMES SEEMS as if the defence of our country
has been quite badly neglected. Until recently, we
never thought about it, and just got on with our business;
but the events of the past few days have got us worried.

I run a shoemaker's on the square in front of the royal
palace. I'd just opened my shop for the morning when
I saw that that every street was guarded by armed men.
They're not our soldiers: it turns out they're nomads
from the north. In some way I can't get my head around,
they've pushed forward into the capital, even though it's
so far from the border. In any case, they're here, and every
morning it looks like there are more of them.

Since they're nomads, they camp under the open sky
and look down on living in houses. They're always busy
sharpening their swords, filing their arrows and practising
on horseback. They've turned this peaceful, painstakingly
clean public square into a stable. We do sometimes try
to go out of our shops to clear away at least the worst
of the mess, but it's a pointless effort and it puts us in

danger of being trampled by the wild horses or injured by their riders' whips.

There's no talking to the nomads. They don't speak our language and barely have one of their own. The noises they use as speech make them sound like crows. All you hear these days is that crow-like croaking. Our way of life, our laws, are incomprehensible to them, and irrelevant. That must be why they're also hostile to any attempt to communicate with sign language. You can talk till you sprain your jaw and gesture till you dislocate your wrists, they won't have understood you and they will never understand you. They often just grimace; then you can see the whites of their eyes rolling and foam spilling out of their mouths, but they're not trying to express anything, nor even to frighten you; they do it just because that's how they are. What they need, they take. You can't really say that they use force. When they appear, you step aside and let them have everything.

They've taken many a good piece from my stores as well. But I can't complain when I see, for example, how bad it is for the butcher across from me. As soon as he brings in any supplies, it's all torn away from him and guzzled by the nomads. Even their horses eat meat; you'll often see a rider lying next to his horse with both of them tucking into the same piece of meat, one from each end. The butcher is too afraid to stop bringing in the deliveries. We understand why, so we've scraped together some money to support him. If the nomads stopped getting their meat, who knows what they'd think of doing; that said, who knows how they'll act even if they do get their meat every day.

The other morning, the butcher thought he could at least save himself the work of chopping up the meat and just had a live ox brought in. He can never do that again. I had to go and lie on the floor at the very back of the workshop for more than an hour, with all my clothes, sheets and pillows piled on top of myself, just so as not to hear the ox's screaming; the nomads jumped on it from all sides and tore out chunks of warm meat with their teeth. It was quiet for a long time before I dared go outside again; they were sprawled around the ox's carcass like drinkers around a barrel of wine.

It was then that I think I saw the king himself at one of the palace windows; he never usually comes to these outer buildings, he lives in the innermost of the palace gardens; but this time—at least this is what I thought I saw—he was standing at one of the windows and looking down, his head bowed, at the commotion in front of his palace.

"How's this going to turn out?" we all ask each other. "How long will we need to endure these burdens and ordeals? The royal palace is what attracted the nomads, but it doesn't know how to drive them away again. The gate stays locked; the guards, who used to have a ceremony of marching in and out, now stay behind barred windows. The job of saving the country has been left to us artisans and business people, but we aren't up to it; we've never claimed to be capable of something like that. It's a misunderstanding, and we're all going to go under because of it."

IN THE PENAL COLONY

"IT'S A UNIQUE PIECE of equipment," said the officer to the travelling researcher, looking over the familiar machinery with an air of admiration. The researcher seemed to have taken up the commandant's invitation only out of politeness; he'd been asked whether he'd like to witness the execution of a soldier who'd been sentenced to death for disobeying and insulting a superior officer. Even in the penal colony there didn't seem to be much interest in this execution. At least, there was no one else here with the officer and the researcher in this steep, sandy little valley enclosed by bare cliffs, apart from the condemned man himself, a stupid-looking, slack-jawed individual with scruffy hair and a dirty face, and a soldier who was holding a heavy chain attached to smaller chains that restrained the condemned man at his wrists, ankles and neck, and that were also connected to one another with an even smaller set of chains. The condemned man looked as submissive as a dog, as if they could have let him wander around the slopes on his own, and would have only needed to whistle for him when they wanted to start the execution.

The researcher wasn't especially interested in this machine and paced up and down behind the condemned man, almost visibly indifferent, while the officer made the final preparations, first creeping under the machine's foundations, which were dug deep into the earth, then climbing a ladder to inspect its uppermost parts. These jobs could have been left to a mechanic, but the officer performed them with great zeal, whether because he was a particular fan of the machine, or because there was some other reason why the work couldn't be entrusted to anyone else. "All right, it's all ready to go," he finally called out, and climbed down off the ladder. He was very out of breath, with his mouth hanging open, and he'd stuffed two ladies' handkerchiefs into the collar of his uniform.

"These uniforms are really too heavy for the tropics," said the researcher, rather than asking about the machine as the officer had expected.

"True," said the officer, washing his oily, grease-covered hands in a bucket of water, "but they're a symbol of home; we don't want to lose our connection to it. — Now have a look at this machine," he added immediately, and dried his hands with a cloth while he pointed at it. "Up to this point, I've had to do some of the work by hand, but from now it'll run automatically." The researcher nodded and followed the officer, who tried to cover himself for all eventualities by saying: "Of course, problems can come up. I hope there won't be any today, but you can never say for certain that they won't. After all, the machine has to operate non-stop for twelve hours. But if problems do come up, they're always very small things that you can easily fix.

"Wouldn't you like to sit down?" he asked in the end, then reached into a jumble of wicker chairs, pulled one out and offered it to the researcher, who felt he couldn't say no. He found himself sitting at the edge of a pit and threw a quick glance into it. The pit wasn't very deep. On one side, the earth that had been dug out was banked up into a rough wall; on the other side stood the machine. "I don't know," said the officer, "whether the commandant has already explained the machine to you?" The researcher made an ambiguous gesture; that was all the officer wanted, because now he could explain the machine himself. "This machine," he said, taking hold of a crank handle and leaning on it, "was invented by our old commandant. I worked with him on the very first trials and was involved in everything until it was completed. But the credit for inventing it is all his. Have you heard much about our old commandant? No? Well, it's not an exaggeration if I tell you that the whole way the colony is organized is his work. When he was on his deathbed, we, his friends, already knew that he'd made the colony's structure so self-enclosed that his successor, even if he arrived with thousands of plans of his own, wouldn't be able to change anything of the old man's, at least not for many years. And our prediction has been borne out; the new commandant has had to recognize that fact. It's a shame you never met the old commandant! — But," the officer interrupted himself, "I'm rambling while the machine stands here waiting in front of us. It consists, as you can see, of three parts. The lower part is called the bed, the upper part is called the engraver and this part suspended in the middle is called the harrow."

"The harrow?" asked the researcher. He hadn't been listening closely; the sun was far too strong in this unshaded valley and he found it difficult to gather his thoughts. It made the officer seem more impressive for carrying on in his tight parade uniform, weighed down with epaulettes and strung with braid, eagerly explaining his work while still making small adjustments here and there with a screwdriver. The soldier on guard looked to be in a similar condition to the researcher. He'd wrapped the chain holding the condemned man around his wrists and was leaning on his rifle, letting his head slump down on his neck and paying no attention to anything. The researcher wasn't surprised; the officer was speaking French and he was certain that neither the soldier nor the condemned man could understand what he was saying. So it was all the more striking that the condemned man was nevertheless trying hard to follow the officer's explanation.

With a kind of sleepy tenacity, he looked wherever the officer was pointing; when the researcher interrupted with a question, both he and the officer turned to look at him.

"Yes, the harrow," said the officer. "It's a fitting name. The needles are arranged like the spikes on a harrow and that's how the whole thing operates, albeit just in one spot and with a much higher degree of sophistication. You'll see what I mean in a moment. The condemned man is laid down here on the bed. — I want to describe the machine before I start the process. Then you'll have a better sense of what's going on. Also, one of the cogs in the engraver is badly worn; it screeches very loudly when it's moving and you can hardly hear yourself think over the noise; unfortunately, it's very difficult to get replacement parts out here. — So, this is the bed, as I was saying. It's completely covered in a layer of cotton wool; you'll soon see why that's needed. The condemned man lies face down on this layer of cotton wool, naked of course; there are restraints for the hands, the feet and the neck—here, here and here—to keep him in place. Here, at the top end of the bed, where the man, as I mentioned, lies face down, there's a block of felt that can be easily adjusted to slip into the man's mouth. It's there to stop him screaming or biting through his tongue. You see, the man has no choice but to take the block into his mouth, because otherwise his neck would be broken by the restraints."

"This is cotton wool?" asked the researcher, and leant forward.

"Yes, absolutely," the officer said with a smile, "feel it for yourself." He took the researcher's hand and moved it across the bed. "It's been specially prepared, that's why it looks a little different than usual; I'll come on to what that's for later on." The researcher had been slightly won over by the machine; shielding his eyes against the sun, he looked up at the top of the apparatus. It was a big construction. The bed and the engraver were the same size and looked like two dark troughs. The engraver was about two metres above the bed; the two parts were connected at the corners by brass poles that shone in the sunshine. Between the two troughs, the harrow was suspended from a steel chain.

The officer had hardly noticed the researcher's previous indifference, but he certainly picked up on his growing interest and paused his explanation to give the researcher more time to examine the machine. The condemned man copied the researcher; since he couldn't put his hand over his eyes, he squinted up at the top of the machine.

"So the man lies there," said the researcher, then leant back in his chair and folded one leg over the other.

"Yes," said the officer, pushing his cap back on his head and wiping his hand down his overheated face. "Now, listen carefully. Both the bed and the engraver are equipped with their own electric battery; the bed needs one for itself, the engraver's is for the harrow. As soon as the man is tightly fastened, the bed starts to move. It vibrates by making tiny, rapid movements from side to side, and up and down. You'll have seen similar equipment in mental hospitals; the difference is that with this machine, every movement has been precisely calculated; each one has to correspond precisely to the movement of the harrow. And it's the harrow that actually carries out the sentence."

"What is the sentence?" asked the researcher.

"You don't know that either?" said the officer in astonishment, and bit his lip. "Excuse me, please, if I've been getting ahead of myself in the explanation; I'm very sorry about that. You see, the commandant used to give the explanation himself; the new commandant has given up that honourable duty; but the idea that he would fail to explain sentencing to such an eminent visitor"—the researcher tried to fend off this compliment with both hands, but the officer insisted on using that phrase— "that he wouldn't even tell such an eminent visitor, that's something new, and it"—he had a curse on the tip of his tongue, but he pulled himself together and just said: "I wasn't told, the fault isn't mine. And as it happens, I'm the person best placed to explain our sentencing because, right here,"—he patted his breast pocket—"I've still got the old commandant's original sketches."

"Sketches by the old commandant himself?" asked the researcher. "Was there anything he couldn't do? Was he really a soldier, a judge, a builder, a chemist and a draughtsman?"

"Yes, indeed," said the officer, nodding with a fixed, pensive expression. He inspected his hands; they didn't strike him as clean enough to touch the sketches, so he went to the bucket and washed them again. Then he pulled out a small leather portfolio and said: "Our sentence doesn't sound particularly severe. The condemned man has the law he has broken written onto his skin with the harrow. This man, for example"—the officer gestured towards him—"will have inscribed onto his skin: Respect your superior officers!"

The researcher glanced across at the condemned man when the officer pointed at him; his head was lowered and he seemed to be straining his ears to try and understand at least some of what was going on. But the shapes he formed with his rubbery lips made clear that he hadn't understood anything at all. The researcher had wanted to put several questions to the officer, but looking at the man, he just asked, "Does he know his sentence?"

"No," said the officer, and was about to carry on with his explanation when the researcher interrupted him: "He doesn't know his own sentence?"

"No," the officer said again, paused for a moment as if to let the researcher clarify his reasons for asking that, then added: "It would be pointless to tell him. He's going to get it written on his own skin."

The researcher would have let it go, but he felt the condemned man look across at him; he seemed to be asking whether the researcher could condone the procedure he'd just had explained. So the researcher, who'd already leant back in his chair, shifted forward again and asked, "But that he's been sentenced for something, surely he knows that?"

"Not that either," said the officer, and smiled at the researcher as if starting to expect peculiar comments from him.

"No," said the researcher, wiping his hand across his forehead. "So this man also doesn't know whether his defence was successful?"

"He hasn't been given an opportunity to defend himself," said the officer, glancing off to the side as if he were speaking to himself and didn't want to embarrass the researcher by telling him such obvious things.

"But he must have had some opportunity to defend himself," said the researcher, and stood up from his chair.

The officer saw the danger that his explanation of the machine's workings would be considerably delayed; he went over to the researcher, took him by the arm and pointed at the condemned man, who, now that he was plainly being discussed, stood to attention while the soldier pulled his chains taut. The officer said, "The way it works is this. I've been appointed judge here in the penal colony. Despite my youth. Because I helped the old commandant on all punishment-related matters and also because I know the machine better than anyone else. The principle on which I make my decisions is this: the defendant's guilt is never in doubt. Other courts can't follow that principle because they have more than one member and they also have higher courts above them. It's not like that here, or at least it wasn't under the old commandant. The new one, admittedly, has shown some signs of wanting to interfere in my court, but I've managed to hold him off so far, and I should be able to keep that up. — You wanted to have this case explained; it's as simple as they all are. This morning, a captain reported that this man, who's assigned to him as a steward and sleeps in front of his door, slept straight through one of his duties. You see, he's supposed to get up on the hour and salute in front of the captain's door. Hardly an onerous duty and certainly a necessary one, because it keeps him fresh both for his guard duty and as a steward. Last night, the captain wanted to check whether this man was discharging his duty properly and found him crouched down, fast asleep. He fetched his riding crop and hit him across the face. Instead of getting up and begging for forgiveness, this man grabbed his superior officer by the legs and shouted: 'Throw away the whip or I'll eat you.' — Those are the facts. The captain came to me an hour ago, I took down his statement and wrote out the judgment. Then I had the man put in chains. It was all very straightforward. If I'd first made the man appear in front of me and questioned him, it would only have created confusion. He would have lied, and if I'd managed to catch him lying, he would have told different lies, and so on. This way I've got him and won't let him go again. — Does that answer your questions? We're running a bit behind, the execution should have begun already, and I haven't finished explaining how the machine works." He urged the researcher to sit back down in the chair, and continued: "As you can see, the harrow matches the shape of a person; this is the harrow for the upper body; these are the harrows for the legs. For the head, there's only this little spike. Is that all clear?" He bent down to the researcher and smiled encouragingly, ready to explain in any amount of detail.

The researcher looked at the harrow with a wrinkled brow. The description of the judicial process hadn't satisfied him. But he said to himself that, after all, this was a penal colony, that special measures were necessary here and that everything had to be handled in a rigorously military fashion. He also placed some hope in the new commandant, who was obviously trying, albeit slowly, to introduce a new system that went beyond the limited thinking of this officer. From out of this train of thought he asked, "Will the commandant attend the execution?"

"It's not certain either way," said the officer, who seemed to find this unexpected question painful, and his friendly expression turned into a grimace. "That's another reason why we've got to get on with it. I'm sorry to say I'll even have to cut short some of the explanation. But tomorrow, once the machine has been cleaned—the fact that it gets so dirty is its only failing—I could fill you in on the details later. But just the essentials for now. — When the man lies on the bed and it has started to shake, the harrow is lowered down to his body. It automatically positions itself so that the tips of the needles are only just touching him; once the set-up is complete, this steel chain locks to become a rod. And then the performance begins. Someone without the necessary background wouldn't notice any difference between different punishments. It looks like the harrow is doing the same job each time. As it shakes, it jabs the tips of the needles into the body, which is also being shaken by the bed. And so you can view the sentence as it's being inscribed, the harrow itself is made of glass. That caused us several technical problems, especially when it came to attaching the needles, but after many attempts we finally managed it. We left no stone unturned. And now anyone can look through the glass to see the sentence being written on the skin. Wouldn't you like to come closer and see the needles for yourself?"

The researcher stood up slowly, went over and bent down to the harrow. "You see," said the officer. "It's actually a pair of needles repeated many times over. Each long one has a short one beside it. The long one inscribes and the short one sprays water to wash away the blood and keep the writing clear. The mixture of blood and water then runs down into these little grooves, which all lead into this drain, and that flows out of the waste pipe into the ditch underneath." With his finger, the officer traced the route that the liquid had to follow. When he, trying to make it as easy as possible to visualize, cupped his hands beneath the waste pipe, the researcher lifted his head away from the machine and, with one hand out behind him, groped his way back into the chair. At that moment, he saw to his horror that the condemned man had also taken up the officer's invitation to have a closer look at the workings of the harrow. He'd tugged the sleepy soldier holding the chain forward a little and was leaning down over the glass. The researcher could see him uncertainly trying to make out whatever the two gentlemen had just been inspecting, but because he hadn't had it explained, he couldn't make any sense of it. He bent over one part and then another. His eyes kept running across the glass harrow. The researcher wanted to shoo him away because what he was doing was probably punishable. But the officer held the researcher back with one hand, picked up a lump of earth with the other and threw it at the soldier. The soldier opened his eyes with a start, saw what the condemned man had dared to do, dropped his rifle, braced the heels of his boots against the ground and yanked him back so hard he immediately fell over, then stood over him as he writhed on the ground, jangling his chains. "Stand him up!" yelled the officer, because he noticed that the researcher was becoming unhelpfully distracted by the condemned man. The researcher even leant past the harrow, not paying it any attention at all, just to see what was happening to him. "Be careful with him," the officer yelled again. He went around the machine, grabbed the man under the armpits himself and, with the soldier's help, finally got him on his feet, even though he kept falling over again.

"So now I understand the whole process," said the researcher when the officer came back to him.

"Apart from the most important thing," said the officer, taking the researcher by the arm and pointing to the top of the machine. "Up there in the engraver is the actual gear train that regulates the harrow's movements; and that gear train is configured to match the drawing of the sentence. As I mentioned, I'm still using the sketches made by the old commandant. Here they are,"—he took several sheets of paper from the leather portfolio—"Unfortunately, I can't let you hold them yourself, they're the most precious thing I have. But please sit down and I'll show them to you from this distance, you'll be able to see everything just fine." He held up the first sheet. The researcher would have liked to say something complimentary, but all he could see were labyrinthine lines criss-crossing each other and covering the paper so thickly it was hard to see any white space at all. "Read it," said the officer.

"I can't," said the researcher.

"But it's perfectly clear."

"It's very elaborate," said the researcher, dodging the demand. "But I'm afraid I can't decipher it."

"Yes," the officer said, then laughed and put the portfolio away again. "It's no primary school calligraphy, that's for sure. You've got to spend a long time reading it. I'm sure you'd be able to see it in the end. Of course, the lettering can't be too simple; after all, it's not supposed to kill at once, on average it takes somewhere in the region of twelve hours; the turning point comes after about six. So there have to be many, many embellishments surrounding the script itself; the actual text only marks the body in quite a narrow band; the rest of the body is for the flourishes. Can you see now why the work of the harrow and the machine is so special? — Look at this!" He jumped onto the ladder, turned a wheel and shouted down: "Watch out, move to the side!" The whole thing started to move. If the wheel hadn't screeched, it would have been magnificent. The officer shook his fist at the screeching wheel as though it were a surprise to him, then spread his arms apologetically towards the researcher and hurriedly climbed back down to watch the machine's motion from the ground. Something only he noticed still wasn't quite right; he climbed back up, reached into the interior of the engraver with both hands, then, instead of using the ladder, quickly slid down one of the poles and, to make himself heard, shouted excitedly into the researcher's ear: "Do you understand the process? The harrow starts writing; once it has finished applying the script to the man's back for the first time, the cotton wool tilts and slowly turns his body to the side, to present a new area to the harrow. Meanwhile, the raw areas are pressed against the cotton wool, which, because of the way it has been prepared, immediately stops the bleeding and prepares the skin so the script can be deepened. Then, when the body is turned again, the prongs at the edge of the harrow, here, rip the cotton wool off the wounds and fling it into the ditch, letting the harrow get back to work. Going back and forth like this, it inscribes the sentence ever more deeply over the course of twelve hours. For the first six, the condemned man lives in much the same way as he did before, except that he's in pain. After two hours, we take the felt block out of his mouth because he won't have the strength to scream any more. Also, here at the head end, we put a kind of warm rice porridge into this electrically heated pot, so that the man can lap it up with his tongue if he wants to. No one has ever passed it up. At least, I've never heard of anyone, and my experience with this is pretty extensive. It's only after around six hours that he'll lose his interest in food. I'll usually be kneeling down here so I can observe this phenomenon. The man rarely swallows his last mouthful, he'll just turn it over in his mouth for a while and finally spit it into the ditch. I've got to be careful, otherwise I'd get sprayed in the face. You'll see how quiet the man gets in the sixth hour! Understanding starts to dawn on even the stupidest ones. It begins around their eyes and spreads out from there. It's a sight that might tempt you to lie down next to him under the harrow. Nothing much happens from then on, just that the man slowly deciphers the script, he purses his lips as if he's listening. You've seen yourself that it's not easy to decipher the script by looking at it; our man deciphers it from his wounds. It's a lot of work; it'll take him another six hours to get it done. At that point, the harrow skewers him completely and tosses him into the ditch, where he slaps down onto the bloody water and the cotton wool. That's the end of the execution and we, the soldier and I, shovel some earth over him."

The researcher had tilted one ear towards the officer and was watching the machine with his hands in his pockets. The condemned man watched it too, but without understanding what it did. He crouched a little and followed the movements of the swinging needles until the soldier, at a signal from the officer, used a knife to cut through his shirt and trousers from behind so they fell off him; he tried to grab at the falling clothes to cover himself, but the soldier lifted him into the air and shook the last scraps of fabric off him. The officer paused the machine and in this new quiet the condemned man was laid down under the harrow. His chains were taken off and replaced with straps; at first, this seemed to strike the condemned man as an improvement. Then the harrow lowered itself a little further, because the man was comparatively thin. When the needles touched him, a shudder ran across his skin; the soldier was busy securing his right hand, but his left stretched out without knowing what for; it happened to reach in the direction of the researcher. The officer watched the researcher constantly from the corner of his eye, as if trying to see what impression the execution, which had been at least superficially explained, was making on him.

The strap for the man's right wrist snapped; the soldier had probably pulled it too tight. The soldier held up the torn strap, asking for help. The officer went over to him and, his face turned towards the researcher, said, "The machine has lots of moving parts, it's inevitable that something rips or breaks from time to time, but you can't let that skew your overall opinion of it. A strap like this we can replace straight away; I'll use a chain instead, even though that'll make the bed's motion a little less smooth for the right arm." And while he fastened the chain, he added: "Our resources for maintaining the machine are very limited these days. Under the old commandant,

I had an unlimited budget solely for repairs. We had a small warehouse where we kept all kinds of replacement parts. I admit that I almost got wasteful with it all, I mean before, not now, whatever the new commandant likes to claim; he'll use anything as a pretext to attack the old way of doing things. These days he oversees the repair budget himself and if I put in a request for a new strap, I have to present the broken one as evidence it's needed, then it'll take ten days for a new one to arrive, and when it does it'll be terrible quality and basically useless. As for how I'm supposed to keep the machine going in the meantime, that's something no one bothers about."

The researcher considered. Intervening in other people's affairs is always a dubious proposition. He was neither a resident of the penal colony nor a citizen of the state to which it belonged. If he wanted to condemn this execution or even try to prevent it, they could have said to him: you're a foreigner here, keep your opinions to yourself. He would have had no response to that; at most he could have added that he was a little surprised by his own behaviour, because the purpose of his travels was to act as an observer and in no way to try and get mixed up in other countries' judicial processes. But in this instance it was very tempting. The injustice of the procedure and the inhumanity of the sentence were beyond doubt. Nobody could have suspected the researcher of having any vested interests, since the man was a stranger to him, not a compatriot of his and not someone who inspired any particular compassion. The researcher himself had arrived with letters of recommendation from the highest officials, had been welcomed here with the greatest respect, and the fact that he had been invited to watch this execution seemed to suggest that he was being asked his opinion of what was going on. That was all the more likely since the commandant, as he'd heard all too clearly, was no supporter of this process and seemed to be treating the officer with something bordering on hostility.

At that moment, he heard the officer give a cry of rage. He had just, not without effort, pushed the felt block into the condemned man's mouth when the latter succumbed to an irresistible nausea, closed his eyes and vomited. The officer hastily tore the block from his mouth and tried to turn the man's head towards the ditch, but it was too late, the vomit had already spattered the machine. "It's all the commandant's fault!" shouted the officer and started wildly rattling one of the brass poles in his fury. "They're making my machine as dirty as a cowshed." With trembling hands, he showed the researcher what had happened. "Haven't I spent hours trying to make the commandant understand that prisoners shouldn't be given anything to eat for a day before the execution? But no, this new mild approach means they have other ideas. Before the man's led away, the commandant's ladies stuff him full of sweets. His whole life, he's lived on stinking fish and now he's got to eat sweets! That's not a catastrophe, I wouldn't complain, but why don't we ever get a new block, something I've spent three months asking for? How could you not be disgusted, putting something in your mouth that more than a hundred men have sucked and bitten on while they died?"

The condemned man was resting his head and looked peaceful; the soldier was busy using the man's shirt to wipe the machine. The officer went over to the researcher who, suspecting something, stepped back a little. But the officer took him by the hand and pulled him aside. "I'd like to have a word with you in confidence," he said, "That's all right, isn't it?"

"Of course," said the researcher, and listened with his eyes lowered.

"This procedure and this execution you've been given the opportunity to admire no longer has any public supporters here in our colony. I'm its only defender, and the only one standing up for the old commandant's legacy. I can no longer hope to develop the procedure any further, it takes all my strength just to preserve what we already have. When the old commandant was still alive, the colony was full of his supporters; I may have some of his powers of persuasion, but I don't have any of his authority; as a result, all his supporters have gone underground, there are still lots of them, but no one admits to it. Today—that is, an execution day—if you go to the tea house and listen in, all you're likely to hear is ambivalent chatter. Those are all supporters, but under the current commandant and given his current attitude, they're completely useless. So I ask you: should the arrival of this commandant and the ladies who influence him mean that a life's work"—he gestured at the machine—"is destroyed? Can you allow that to happen? Even if you're a foreigner who's only spending a few days on our island? Believe me, there's no time to lose; they're already concocting an attack on my judicial authority; they hold discussions I'm not invited to in the commandant's office; even your visit today is typical of the whole situation; they're cowards and so they prefer to send you, a stranger, in their place. — You should have seen how different the executions were in the old days! A day before the execution had even started, this valley would be full of people; everyone came to watch; the commandant and his ladies would appear early in the morning; the camp was woken with fanfares; I reported that everything was ready; the colony's best people—not one senior official would miss it—arranged themselves nearest to the machine; this pile of chairs is a miserable remnant from that time. The machine would be gleaming, freshly polished: I'd use some replacement parts for almost every execution. In front of hundreds of pairs of eyes—the spectators would be standing on tiptoe all the way to the cliffs—the condemned man would be laid under the harrow by the commandant himself. The work that these days is done by a common soldier was assigned to me, the president of the court, and was considered an honour. And then the execution began! There was no screeching to disturb the smooth running of the machine. Some people didn't even watch, just lay there in the sand with their eyes closed; but they all knew: justice is being done. In the hush all you could hear was the groaning of the condemned man, muffled by the block. These days the machine can't even elicit any groans that the block won't stifle; back then, the writing needles discharged an acid that we're not allowed to use any more. Well, and then the sixth hour came around! It was always impossible to find room for everyone who wanted to watch from close up. The commandant, with his usual wisdom, ordered the children to be let through; for my part, I got to be there because of my duties; I'd often be sitting right there with a small child in each arm. How attentively we watched the transfiguration of their tormented expressions; how close we kept our own faces to the splendour of that justice, which was already fleeting in the moment it was finally achieved! What good times, old friend!" The officer had plainly forgotten who was standing in front of him; he'd put his arm around the researcher and rested his head on the researcher's shoulder. The researcher was extremely embarrassed and impatiently looked past the officer to the others. The soldier had finished cleaning up and was pouring more rice porridge from a can into the bowl. As soon as the condemned man noticed this—he seemed to have completely recovered—he again began to slurp up the porridge with his tongue. The soldier kept pushing him away, because the porridge was meant for later on, but he didn't seem to be behaving properly either as he scooped up the prisoner's porridge with his dirty hands and ate it himself.

The officer quickly got a grip on himself. "I wasn't trying to influence you emotionally," he said. "I know it's impossible to make someone now understand what those times were like. And after all, the machine's work continues and it speaks for itself. It speaks for itself even if there's no one else here. And at the end, the body will still make its strangely gentle descent into the ditch, even if there are no longer hundreds of flies gathering around it like there used to be. Back then, we had to put up a handrail around the ditch; it's long gone now."

The researcher wanted to turn his face away from the officer, and looked around aimlessly. The officer thought he was looking at the empty valley; he took the researcher's hands, moved round to catch his eye, and asked, "So you can feel it, then, what a disgrace this is?"

But the researcher said nothing. The officer left him alone for a moment. With his legs wide apart, his hands on his hips, he stayed quiet and stared at the ground. Then he gave the researcher an encouraging smile and said, "I was standing nearby yesterday when the commandant invited you to watch. I heard the invitation. I know the commandant. I understood the point of the invitation right away. Although he is actually powerful enough to act against me, he doesn't dare, and instead he wants to expose me to the judgment of a respected outsider like yourself. It's very calculating of him; this is your second day on the island, you didn't know the old commandant or his thinking, you're imbued with European attitudes, you might even be a principled opponent of the death penalty and especially of this kind of execution by machine; moreover, you're watching this execution be carried out without any public participation, sadly, on a run-down machine—and taking all these things together (this is how the commandant thinks), isn't it very possible that you would disapprove of this process? And if you did disapprove of it (I'm still speaking about how the commandant thinks), perhaps you wouldn't keep that to yourself, because you presumably have faith in your well-honed convictions. You must have seen many idiosyncrasies among many different peoples and learnt to be respectful, so you probably won't speak out with full force against this process in the way you would at home. But the commandant doesn't even need you to do that. If you just said something in passing, one careless phrase, that would be enough. It wouldn't even need to express what you really think as long as it seemed to correspond to his ideas. He'll question you with all the cunning he can muster, I've got no doubt of that, and his ladies will sit in a circle around you with their ears pricked up. You might say, for example, 'In my country, the judicial process is rather different,' or 'In my country, the accused is examined before sentencing,' or 'Our prisoners are allowed to know their sentence,' or 'We have several punishments other than the death penalty,' or 'We only had torture till the Middle Ages.' All these comments are absolutely correct, and to you seem like innocent, matter-of-fact statements that don't touch on my work here. But how will the commandant react to them? I can see him now, the good commandant, quickly pushing his chair aside and hurrying out onto the balcony; I can see his ladies streaming after him; I can hear him talking—his ladies say he has a voice like thunder—and what he'll say is: 'An eminent Western researcher studying judicial systems around the world has just said that our traditional way of doing things is inhumane. Having heard this opinion from such a prominent expert, I can naturally no longer allow that process to continue. I hereby decree, with immediate effect, that…' and so on. You'll want to intervene, you didn't say what he's announcing, you didn't call my process inhumane, on the contrary, because of your deep insight you think it's the most humane and most dignified you've ever seen, and you also admire the actual machinery—but it's too late; you can't even get out onto the balcony, which is packed with his ladies; you want to raise a protest; you want to shout; but a lady's hand holds your mouth shut—and I and the old commandant's work will be lost."

The researcher had to suppress a smile: so it would be that easy to complete the task he'd thought would be so difficult. He said evasively, "You're overestimating my influence; the commandant has read my letter of recommendation, he knows that I'm not an expert in legal procedures. If I expressed an opinion, it would just be the opinion of a private individual, with no more weight behind it than anyone else's, and anything I said would certainly count for much less than the commandant's opinion, since, as far as I understand it, he has very far-reaching powers here in this penal colony. And if his mind is made up in the way you think, then I'm afraid the end has come for this process, regardless of any opinion from me."

Had the officer understood yet? No, he hadn't. He vehemently shook his head, glanced at the condemned man and the soldier—who both jumped and stopped eating the porridge—went up very close to the researcher, not looking him in the eye but staring at some point on his jacket, and said more quietly than before: "You don't know the commandant; your view of him and all of us here is bound to be—forgive me for saying so—a little naïve. Believe me, your influence here can't be overstated. I was happy when I heard that only you were going to watch the execution. That order of the commandant's was supposed to hurt me, but now I'm turning it to my own advantage. You haven't been distracted by any lying whispers or critical expressions—which would be unavoidable if there was a bigger audience for this execution—you've listened to my explanation, you've seen the machine and you're about to watch the execution itself. You've probably already formed your opinion, but if you have any niggling doubts, I'm sure that watching the execution will put them to rest. So I ask you: help me with the commandant."

The researcher didn't let him go on any further. "How can I?" he exclaimed. "That's impossible. I can't help you any more than I could do you harm."

"You can," said the officer. The researcher noticed to his alarm that the officer had clenched his fists. "You can," said the officer again, even more insistently. "I have a plan that is sure to work. You believe that you don't have enough influence. I know that you do. And even if you were right, shouldn't we try anything we can to preserve this procedure, even if it turns out not to be enough? So listen to my plan. For it to work, it's important above all that for the rest of the day you give away as little as possible about what you think of the machine. If no one asks you directly, don't offer any opinion; anything you do say has to be terse and ambiguous; you want them to get the impression that it's hard for you to talk about it, that it has left you feeling bitter, that if you said something, you would have to lash out with all kinds of criticisms. I'm not asking you to lie; not at all; you should just give short replies like, 'Yes, I saw the execution,' or 'Yes, I heard all the explanations.' That's it, nothing more. And after all, there's more than enough reason for you to feel bitter, even if not in the way the commandant will assume. He'll misunderstand completely and think that you agree with him. That's where my plan comes in. Tomorrow, there's a big meeting of all the senior officials, chaired by the commandant. As you'd expect, he has managed to turn those meetings into a piece of theatre. He's had a gallery built for spectators, which is always full. I've got no choice about taking part in the discussions, even though they make me shudder with disgust. Now, there's no doubt you'll be invited to the meeting; if you stick to my plan for the rest of the day, instead of just inviting you they'll be pleading and insisting. If, for some unforeseeable reason, you're not invited, you'll have to ask for an invitation; there's no question that you'll get one. So tomorrow you'll be sitting in the commandant's box, next to his ladies. He'll keep glancing up to reassure himself that you're there. After a few meaningless and absurd points of debate staged for the spectators—usually about developing the port, it's always about port development!—they'll start talking about the judicial process. If the commandant doesn't move things in that direction, or doesn't do it soon enough, I'll make sure that it happens. I'll stand up and make my report about today's execution. Very short, just to say that it has taken place. My report isn't usually like that, but it will be this time. The commandant will thank me, as always, with a friendly smile and then, he won't be able to help himself, he'll grasp the opportunity. 'We've just heard,' that's what he'll say, or something like it, 'We've just heard an account of yesterday's execution. I would just like to add that this execution was watched by the great researcher and judicial expert who, as you all know, is currently doing us the honour of a visit. This meeting today also has an extra significance because he has decided to join us. Shouldn't we ask this great expert for his impressions of our traditional mode of execution and the legal procedure leading up to it?' Of course there'll be applause from all sides, a general consensus; I'll be the loudest. The commandant will bow to you and say, 'Then, on behalf of everyone here, please do tell us what you think.' At that point, you step up to the railing. Make sure you place your hands where everyone can see them, otherwise the ladies will start playing with your fingers. — And now, finally, it'll be your moment to speak. I don't know how I'm going to get through the hours before it's time. In your speech, you shouldn't hold back in any way, be noisy with the truth, lean forward over the railing, shout, yes, shout your opinion, your unshakeable opinion, at the commandant. But perhaps you won't want to do that, it's not in your character, perhaps in your country people behave differently in these situations, that's fine too, that'll do perfectly, whisper your opinion so that only the officials right beneath you can hear it, you won't even have to mention the lack of spectators at the execution, the screeching wheel, the broken strap, the disgusting block of felt, no, I'll take care of all that, and believe me, if what I say doesn't send him running out of the hall, it'll force him to his knees till he has to pay homage: old commandant, I bow down before you. — That's my plan; will you help me carry it out? But of course you will; more than that, you have to." The officer grabbed the researcher by both arms and, breathing heavily, stared him in the face. He'd yelled the last few phrases so loudly that even the soldier and the condemned man had begun to pay attention; they couldn't understand anything but they left off the food and, still chewing, looked over at the researcher.

His answer to the officer was never in doubt; he'd seen too much over his lifetime to have wobbled on this question; he was fundamentally honest and not afraid. Nevertheless, he hesitated for a moment under the gaze of the officer and the condemned man. But finally he said, as he had to: "No." The officer blinked several times, but didn't look away. "Would you like an explanation?" asked the researcher. The officer nodded silently. "I am opposed to this process," said the researcher. "Even before you took me into your confidence—I won't break that confidence in any way—I'd already considered whether I would be justified in intervening to try and stop this and whether an intervention would have even the smallest chance of success. It was clear to me who I should turn to: the commandant, of course. You've made that clearer still, but don't think that you've confirmed what I intended to do, on the contrary, I'm deeply touched by your sincere conviction, even if I won't be diverted by it."

The officer stayed mute, turned to the machine, took hold of one of the brass poles and then looked up at the engraver, leaning back a little, as if he wanted to check that everything was in order. The soldier and the condemned man seemed to have struck up some kind of friendship; even though it was difficult because he was so tightly bound, the condemned man made hand signals to the soldier, who bent down to him; the condemned man whispered something; the soldier nodded.

The researcher followed the officer and said, "You don't know what I'm going to do. Yes, I will tell the commandant what I think of this process, but not at the meeting, I'll tell him privately; I also won't stay here long enough to get pulled into a public debate; I'll set off early tomorrow morning, or at least be on a ship by then."

The officer didn't seem to be listening. "So you didn't find the judicial process convincing," he said to himself and gave a smile like an old man hearing nonsense from a child and keeping his real thoughts concealed behind it.

"That means it's time," he said finally, and suddenly looked up at the researcher, bright-eyed, as if trying to communicate some request, some demand that he take part.

"What's it time for?" the researcher asked uneasily, but didn't get a reply.

"You're free to go," the officer said to the condemned man in his own language. The man didn't believe him to begin with. "Yes, you're free to go," said the officer. For the first time, the condemned man's face really became animated. Was it true? Was it just some passing whim of the officer's? Had the foreign researcher secured his release? What was going on? These questions played across his face. But not for long. Whatever the reasons, if he was allowed to be free, he wanted to be free for real, and he began to pull at his restraints as much as the harrow would permit.

"You'll tear the strap!" shouted the officer. "Keep still! We're letting you out." He signalled to the soldier and together they started undoing the straps. The condemned man laughed wordlessly to himself, now turning left to face the officer, now right towards the soldier, and not leaving out the researcher either.

"Pull him out," the officer told the soldier. It needed to be done quite carefully because of the harrow. The condemned man already had some cuts on his back because of his impatience.

From that point on, the officer barely paid any attention to him. He went over to the researcher, pulled out his leather portfolio again, eventually found the page he was looking for, and showed it to the researcher. "Read it," he said.

"I can't," said the researcher. "I already told you that I can't read these pages."

"Look closer," the officer said, and stood next to the researcher to read with him. When that didn't help either, he pointed with his pinkie finger, from high above the page, as if it must never be touched, and moved it across the page to help the researcher read the script. The researcher did make an effort, hoping that he'd be able to do at least one thing to please the officer, but he found it impossible. So the officer began to draw the letters and then finally he read them all out together: "'Be just!' is what it says," he told the researcher, "Now you must be able to see it." The researcher bent so far forward over the page that the officer moved it further away for fear he would touch it; although the researcher didn't say anything else, it was obvious that he still hadn't been able to read it. "'Be just!' is what it says," the officer repeated.

"That's fine," said the researcher. "I don't doubt that that's right."

"All right, then," the officer said, at least partially satisfied, and climbed up the ladder holding the page in one hand; he very carefully placed the sheet in the engraver and then seemed to be completely reconfiguring the gear train; it was difficult work, the gears must be very small; sometimes the officer had to examine them so closely that his head disappeared entirely into the engraver.

The researcher followed this work from below; his neck grew stiff and his eyes began to hurt with the brightness of the sky. The soldier and the condemned man were busy with each other. The soldier used his bayonet to pull the man's shirt and trousers out of the ditch. The shirt was horribly filthy and the condemned man washed it in the water bucket. When he put the things on, he and the soldier both roared with laughter, because the clothes were still cut through at the back. The condemned man seemed to feel obliged to entertain the soldier and he twirled around in his shredded clothes in front of him, while the soldier laughed so hard he sat on the ground and slapped his thighs. Nevertheless, they did try to restrain themselves a little because of the two gentlemen.

Once the officer had finally finished at the top of the machine, he took another look over the whole thing, smiled, flipped the engraver's lid shut, climbed down, glanced into the pit, then at the condemned man, was satisfied to see that he'd fished out his clothes, went over to the water bucket to wash his hands, noticed the disgusting filth too late, was sad that he now couldn't wash his hands, and—it wasn't much of a substitute but better than nothing—plunged them into the sand, before standing up and starting to unbutton his uniform. The two ladies' handkerchiefs that he'd stuffed into his collar fell into his hand. "Here you have your handkerchiefs," he said and threw them to the condemned man. To the researcher he said in explanation: "A present from the ladies."

Despite the evident hurry with which he took off his tunic and then undressed fully, he still handled every item of clothing with great care, even running his fingers across the silver braid on his jacket and shaking a tassel into place. What didn't really fit with this carefulness, however, was that as soon as he'd finished folding a piece of clothing, he reluctantly tossed it into the ditch. The last thing he had left was his short sword and the belt it hung from. He pulled the sword out of the scabbard, snapped it, gathered everything together—the pieces of sword, the scabbard and the belt—and threw it all down so it jangled at the bottom of the ditch.

Now he stood there naked. The researcher bit his lip and said nothing. He knew what was going to happen, but he had no right to prevent the officer from doing anything he'd decided to. If the judicial process the officer was so devoted to really was about to be halted—possibly as a result of intervention by the researcher, something he still felt he had to do—then the officer's behaviour was entirely correct; in his place the researcher would have acted no differently.

The soldier and the condemned man didn't understand right away; they weren't even watching to begin with. The condemned man was delighted to have the handkerchiefs back, but he didn't get to enjoy them for long, because the soldier quickly snatched them out of his hand. The man tried to pull them back out of the soldier's belt, where he'd tucked them in, but the soldier was on his guard. So they squabbled, half joking. Only when the officer was completely naked did they start to pay attention. The condemned man in particular seemed struck by a sense that a great reversal of fortunes was taking place. What had happened to him was now happening to the officer. Perhaps the process would be carried through· to its conclusion. The foreign researcher had probably given the order. This was his revenge. Although he himself hadn't been made to suffer to the end, he was going to be avenged in full. An expression of broad, silent laughter appeared on his face, and didn't fade.

The officer, for his part, had turned to the machine. Although it had been obvious enough beforehand how well he knew its workings, now it was almost upsetting to see how lovingly he handled it and how eagerly it obeyed. He just put his hand near the harrow and it adjusted itself until it found the right height to receive him; he barely touched the side of the bed and it immediately began to tremble; the block of felt approached his mouth, it was clear the officer didn't really want it, but his hesitation only lasted a moment, then he acquiesced and opened his mouth. Everything was ready except that the straps were still hanging loose down the machine's sides, but it seemed they weren't needed, the officer didn't need to be restrained. Then the condemned man noticed the loose straps; in his view the execution wasn't being performed properly if the straps weren't done up; he waved at the soldier and together they went to strap the officer in. The officer had been stretching out his foot to kick the lever that set the engraver in motion; when he saw these two coming, he pulled back his foot and let himself be tied down. But now he couldn't reach the lever any more; neither the soldier not the condemned man would be able to find it; and the researcher had decided not to move a muscle. It turned out not to be necessary; as soon as the straps had been tightened, the machine went into operation; the bed shook, the needles danced on his skin; the harrow swooped down and up. The researcher had been staring for a while when he remembered that one of the gears in the engraver should have been screeching; but everything was quiet, there wasn't even a hum from the machine.

It was so quiet that he was able to take in what else was going on. The researcher looked over at the soldier and the condemned man. The condemned man was the livelier of the two, everything about the machine interested him and he bent down over it, or stretched up to see the higher parts, and he kept pointing his finger to show things to the soldier. The researcher found it painful to watch. He was determined to stay till the end, but he couldn't have stood the sight of these two for long. "Go home," he told them. The soldier might have been ready to leave, but the condemned man seemed to consider the order to be a punishment. He begged to be allowed to stay, bringing his hands together in supplication, and when the researcher shook his head and refused to relent, the condemned man got down on his knees. The researcher saw that orders would do no good here, he would have to go over and chase them away. At that moment, he heard a noise from the engraver. He looked across. Was the gear playing up after all? But it was something else. The engraver's lid rose slowly and eventually flipped completely open. You could see the teeth on one of the gears, which lifted itself up until the whole wheel was in sight; it was as if some force were squeezing the engraver so that there was no space left inside for the gear; it kept turning until it reached the edge of the engraver, then fell, rolled a short distance in the sand and toppled over. But another one was already rising out of the top, and it was followed by many more, big, small, some practically identical; the same happened with all of them; each time it seemed that the engraver must now be empty, but then another especially numerous group of gears appeared, rose out of the box, fell to the ground, rolled in the sand and toppled over. Watching this, the condemned man forgot that the researcher had ordered him to leave; the gears fascinated him, he kept wanting to touch them, and called the soldier to help him, but then pulled his hand back in fright, because another gear popped out and scared him as it rolled closer.

The researcher, on the other hand, was deeply disconcerted; the machine was obviously shaking itself apart; its smooth operation was an illusion; he felt he had to take over since the officer could no longer look after himself. But he hadn't been watching the rest of the machine while the gears were falling; now that the last of them seemed to have left the engraver, the researcher got another, worse surprise. The harrow wasn't writing, only stabbing; and the bed wasn't rolling the officer's body, only lifting it trembling into the needles. The researcher wanted to intervene, maybe stop the whole thing: this wasn't the torture the officer had wanted, this was simple murder. He reached out his hands. But the harrow was already lifting the skewered body to the side, as it usually only did after twelve hours. Blood was streaming from a hundred wounds (unmixed with water; the little tubes had also failed). And now the final stage also malfunctioned: the body didn't drop from the needles, just hung over the ditch, pouring out blood, without dropping. The harrow tried to return to its original position but, as if noticing that it was still carrying this weight, it stayed above the ditch. "Help me!" the researcher shouted to the soldier and the condemned man, and took hold of the officer's feet. He wanted to push from the feet while the other two pushed from the officer's head, so they could slowly slide him off the needles. But the other two couldn't make up their minds to come; the condemned man turned away; the researcher had to go over to them and force them to attend to the officer's head. There, almost against his will, he saw the corpse's face. It was like it had been in life (there was no sign of the promised redemption); what all the others had found in the machine, the officer hadn't; his lips were pressed together, his eyes open, alive-looking, his expression calm and assured, and through his forehead protruded the tip of the big iron spike.

When the researcher, with the soldier and the condemned man following him, reached the first buildings of the colony, the soldier pointed at one of them and said, "That's the tea house."

On the ground floor of this building was a deep, low-ceilinged, cave-like room with walls and ceiling blackened by smoke. One whole side was open to the street. Although the tea house was little different from the colony's other buildings, which, except for the commandant's palatial headquarters, were all fairly run down, it still evoked a sense of history in the researcher and he felt the draw of a previous era. He walked up to it, followed by his two companions, went past the unoccupied tables that stood on the street outside, and breathed in the cool, musty air that came from the interior. "The old man is buried here," said the soldier. "The priest wouldn't let him have a spot in the graveyard. For a while, no one could decide where to bury him and eventually he was buried here. That's something the officer definitely didn't tell you anything about, because that's what he was most ashamed of. A few times, he even came here at night and tried to dig up the old man, but they always chased him away."

"Where is the grave?" asked the researcher, who couldn't believe what the soldier was saying. Right away, both of them, the soldier and the condemned man, went ahead of him and pointed to where the grave was supposed to be. They led the researcher over to the back wall, where customers were sitting at a few of the tables. They were probably dock workers, strong men with gleaming black beards. None of them had a jacket, their shirts were tattered, they were a poor, beaten-down people. When the researcher came close, some of them stood up, pressed themselves against the walls and stared at him. "He's a foreigner," they whispered around the researcher, "he wants to see the grave." They pushed one of the tables aside and underneath it there really was a gravestone. It was a simple stone, small enough to be hidden under a table. It carried an inscription in very small lettering; the researcher had to kneel down to read it. It said: 'Here lies the old commandant. His followers, who are now nameless, dug this grave and placed this stone. There is a prophecy that, after a certain number of years, the old commandant will rise again and lead his followers from this house to wrest back control of the colony. Be faithful, and wait for him!' When the researcher had read this and straightened up, he saw the men standing all around him and grinning, as if they'd read the inscription beside him, found it ridiculous and wanted him to share their opinion. The researcher acted as if he hadn't noticed, gave out a few coins, waited until the table had been pushed back over the grave, left the tea house and walked down to the harbour.

The soldier and the condemned man were held up by meeting some acquaintances in the tea house. But they must have torn themselves away quickly, because the researcher was still only on the long set of stairs that led down to the boats when they came after him. They probably wanted to force him to take them with him. While the researcher spoke to one of the boatmen about being ferried across to the steamship, the two of them raced down the steps, silently, because they didn't dare shout. But by the time they reached the bottom, the researcher was already in the boat and the boatman was pushing off from the shore. They could still have jumped into the boat, but the researcher picked up a heavy, knotted rope, threatened them with it and prevented them from jumping.

THE NEXT VILLAGE

M Y GRANDFATHER used to say: "Life is astonishingly short. When I look back now, it all seems so squashed together that I can hardly understand how a young person could, say, decide to ride to the next village without being afraid—even without any unlucky accidents—that the span of a normal, happy life would not be nearly long enough for him to get there."

A FIRST HEARTACHE

A TRAPEZE VIRTUOSO—whose discipline, practised high in the vaulted domes of the great variety theatres, is famously among the most difficult of any that people can aspire to—had arranged his life in such a way that, initially out of a striving for perfection, then out of increasingly tyrannical habit, he stayed on his trapeze day and night for as long as an engagement lasted. His modest needs were catered to by a rota of attendants who were posted below and hauled everything up and down in specially made containers. The way he lived didn't create many problems for those around him; it was a little distracting to have him up there during the other acts and, although he mostly stayed quiet, a few glances would nevertheless stray up to him from here and there in the audience. But the producers forgave him that because he was an extraordinary, irreplaceable artist. And of course they also understood that he wasn't doing it on a whim, that this was his only means of staying in constant training, of keeping his art at its peak.

It wasn't unhealthy up there and when the weather was warm and the side windows were flung open all round the dome, letting fresh air and strong sunshine pour into the shadowy room, it could be lovely. True, his human contact was very limited; only sometimes did a fellow acrobat climb up to him on a rope ladder; then they'd both sit on the trapeze, leaning against the ropes on each side and chatting. Or some workmen fixing the roof would exchange a few words with him through an open window. Or a fireman checking the emergency lighting on the top floor shouted up one or two respectful, but barely audible, phrases. Other than that, it was quiet around him; from time to time, some stagehand who'd wandered into the empty theatre in the afternoon would glance up thoughtfully into the distant heights where the trapeze artist was practising or resting, unaware that he was being watched.

The trapeze artist could have quietly lived like this had it not been for the unavoidable transfers from venue to venue, which badly disrupted his peace of mind. His manager did try to make sure that the artist's discomfort was kept to a minimum: when they travelled within a city they used sports cars, ideally at night or in the earliest hours of morning, and raced through the empty streets at top speed, albeit still too slowly for the trapeze artist; on trains they would book an entire compartment, where the trapeze artist could spend the journey up in the luggage rack, an admittedly miserable approximation of his usual life, but better than nothing; in the new venues, the trapeze would be set up long before the artist arrived; all the doors leading to the stage were held open, all the corridors kept clear—and yet, the sweetest moments in the manager's life were when the trapeze artist set foot on the rope ladder and, before you knew it, was finally hanging from his trapeze again.

No matter how many transfers the manager successfully handled, each new one was still stressful, because aside from anything else, it wore away at the artist's nerves.

And once, they were travelling together again, the trapeze artist up in the luggage rack, his manager leaning against the window in the opposite corner and reading a book, when the artist spoke to him quietly. The manager was immediately attentive. The artist, biting his lip, said that from now on, instead of just one trapeze, he would need two for his performances, two trapezes opposite each other. The manager agreed at once. But the artist, as if to show that his manager's agreement was as meaningless as any opposition would have been, said that from now on he would never, under any circumstances, perform on a single trapeze. Just the idea that it might happen again seemed to make him shudder. Once again, cautiously and on alert, his manager said that he was in full agreement, that two trapezes were better than one, and that this new arrangement would bring lots of other advantages, such as allowing more variety in the performances. At that, the trapeze artist burst into tears. Deeply shocked, his manager jumped up and asked what on earth had happened; and since he got no response, he climbed onto the seats, stroked the artist and pressed his face against the artist's, so that his own cheeks were wet with the artist's tears. But it was only after many questions and lots of soothing talk that the artist said through his sobs: "Only ever that one bar in my hands—how can I live like that?" After that it was easier for his manager to console him: he promised that he would telegraph ahead from the very next station and arrange the second trapeze; he blamed himself for having let the artist work on a single trapeze for so long, and thanked and praised him for having eventually pointed out his manager's mistake. In this way, he gradually succeeded in reassuring the trapeze artist, and after a while he was able to go back to his corner. But the manager was not reassured; in grave concern he secretly watched the trapeze artist over the top of his book. Once these kinds of thoughts had begun to gnaw at him, could they ever stop again? Wouldn't they just keep getting worse? Weren't they a threat to everything about how he lived? And as the manager watched over the apparently peaceful sleep that the trapeze artist had fallen into once he'd stopped crying, he really thought he could see the first wrinkles beginning to etch themselves into the artist's boyishly smooth forehead.

A REPORT FOR
AN ACADEMY

G ENTLEMEN, eminent members of the academy!
You have done me the honour of asking me to
present a report on my simian past.

Unfortunately, however, I won't be able to carry out
that request in the sense in which it was intended. Nearly
five years now separate me from my simian state, a short
time when measured by the calendar, but practically
endless if you galloped through it like I did, sometimes
accompanied by admirable people, by advice, acclaim
and orchestral music, but fundamentally alone, because
anyone accompanying me, to pursue my metaphor, stayed
safely offstage in the orchestra's pit. That effort would
have been impossible if I'd stubbornly tried to cling on
to my origins, to memories of my youth. In fact, my
highest law was to relinquish any wilfulness I found
within myself; I, a free ape, bent my neck to that yoke.
As a result, whatever memories I had became ever more
closed off from me. Although at first I could still—had

the humans wished it— have gone back through the high, wide arch that the sky forms over the earth, the way back became lower and narrower the more I drove my development forward; I started to feel more comfortable and more embedded in the human world; the storm chasing me from out of my past began to settle; today it's no more than a breeze to cool my heels; the distant gap through which it comes and through which I once came has shrunk so small that even if I had the strength and the willpower to get back to it, I would have to scrape the hide off my body just to squeeze through. To put it frankly, even though I do like to use figures of speech for these things, to put it frankly: your own simian heritage, gentlemen, insofar as you have something like that in your past, is no more remote from you than mine is from me. Yet everyone who walks this earth feels that little tickle at his heel, from a little chimpanzee to the great Achilles.

But I can perhaps answer your invitation in a more limited sense, and will do so with great pleasure. The first thing I learnt was: shake hands; shaking hands leads to openness; and now that I'm at the high point of my career, I'd like to add some candid speech to that first frank handshake. I won't be able to tell the academy anything substantively new and I will fall far short of what was asked of me, which I wouldn't be able to provide with the best will in the world—nevertheless, let me sketch the course of how someone born an ape was able to enter the human world and thrive in it. But even the little that follows I wouldn't be willing to explain if I weren't completely sure of myself and my position, and if I hadn't unshakeably established myself on every great variety stage in the civilized world.

I come from the Gold Coast. For an account of how I was captured I have to rely on the reports of others. A hunting expedition mounted by the Hagenbeck Company—with whose leader I've since shared many a fine bottle of claret—was waiting in a riverbank hide when I and the rest of my troop arrived for an evening drink. Shots were fired; I was the only one hit, and I was hit twice.

Once in the cheek; that one just glanced me, but it left me with a big hairless red scar that earned me the disgusting and wholly unsuitable name Red Peter, which really might have been dreamt up by an ape and which implied that the only difference between me and a recently deceased, moderately well-known performing ape called Peter was the red mark on my cheek. That's just by the by.

The second shot struck me below the hip. It was more serious, that's why I still limp a little to this day. I recently read in a piece by one of the ten thousand windbags who air their opinions of me in the newspapers that my simian nature has not yet been entirely suppressed; the proof being that, when I have visitors, I still like to pull down my trousers to show them where that shot hit me.

That hack deserves to have every finger on his writing hand shot off one at a time. I, *I* can pull down my trousers in front of whomever I please; you'd find nothing but a well-groomed pelt and a scar left by—let me use this specific word for this specific situation, because I don't want to be misunderstood—the scar left by a criminal assault. All this is in the open; there's nothing to hide; any high-minded person would drop the constraints of politeness when it's a matter of demonstrating the truth. If, on the other hand, that scribbler were to pull down his trousers when he had visitors, it would appear in a very different light, and I take it as a sign of vestigial good sense that he doesn't do it. But I'd like him to spare me his delicacy of feeling!

After those shots I came round—and this is where my own memories gradually take over—in a cage below decks on the Hagenbeck steamer. It wasn't the classic cage with four barred sides; rather, it was three-sided and fixed to a crate, with the crate making a wall. It was too low to stand up in and too narrow to sit down. So I crouched with bent, shaking knees and, probably because at first I wanted to stay in the dark and not see anyone, I faced the crate while the thin bars behind me cut into my flesh. It's considered good practice to keep wild animals in this kind of accommodation during their first moments in captivity, and after my experiences I can't now deny that from the human perspective that is correct.

Back then I couldn't think like that. For the first time in my life, I didn't have a way out; at least there was no way out directly ahead of me; directly ahead of me was the crate, with each board nailed firmly to the next. There was in fact one small gap between them, something I greeted with rapturous howls of unreason when I first discovered it, but which was not nearly big enough to fit even just my tail through and which all my simian strength was unable to widen.

I was told later that I made unusually little noise, leading the hunters to conclude that either I would soon give up the ghost or, if I managed to survive the difficult first phase, I would take very well to training. I survived the first phase. Muted sobbing, painful searches for fleas, weary licking of coconuts, knocking my skull against the crate, sticking out my tongue when someone came—these were the first occupations of my new life. But all of them came with the same feeling: no way out. Of course I now only have human words to sketch an ape's emotions, but even if I can no longer precisely describe the old simian truths, the gist is correct, there's no doubt about that.

Until that moment I had always had so many ways out, and now I had none. I'd been run to ground. I would have been no less free if I'd been nailed to the floor. Why was that? Scratch the flesh between your toes until it starts to bleed, and you still won't understand. Push yourself backwards against the bars until they almost cut you in two, and you won't understand. I had no way out, but I had to make myself one, because I couldn't live without it. To be pressed up against that crate for the foreseeable—it would have been the end of me. For Hagenbeck, however, the place for apes was next to that crate—so I ceased to be an ape. A lucid, beautiful deduction, one that I must have somehow gestated in my stomach, because apes think with their bellies.

I'm afraid it will be hard to understand exactly what I mean by a way out. I'm using the term in its most everyday and fullest sense. I'm intentionally not saying freedom. I don't mean that magnificent feeling of having freedom all around you. I may have known it as an ape and I've met humans who long for it. For my part, I've never demanded freedom, neither then nor now. Incidentally, for humans the idea of freedom is all too often a means of deceiving themselves. And although freedom is among the most exalted of feelings, so is the illusion of freedom among the most exalted of illusions. Often in variety shows, while waiting to go on, I've seen some pair of performers doing their work on the trapeze. They swing about, they rock back and forth, they jump around, they glide into each other's arms. I saw one hold the other by clamping her hair in his mouth. 'This is another example of human freedom,' I thought, 'movement as self-congratulation.' What a mockery of sacred nature! A troop of apes would have laughed hard enough to blow down the building.

No, I didn't want freedom. Just a way out; right, left, wherever; I wanted nothing else; even if the way out proved to be an illusion, what I wanted was modest, the illusion would not be any bigger. Onwards, onwards! Anything but to stand still, arms lifted, pressed against the side of a crate.

Today I see clearly that I could never have got away if I hadn't had the greatest inner calm. It's quite possible that I owe everything I've become to the calm that came over me after the first few days on board. And that calm I owe, in turn, to the people on that ship.

They are good people, in spite of everything. To this day I still fondly remember the noise of their heavy footsteps echoing in my half-sleep. They were in the habit of doing everything extremely slowly. If one of them wanted to rub his eyes, he lifted his hand as if it were a dumbbell. Their jokes were crude but cheerful. Their laughter always came mixed with a coughing that sounded dangerous but meant nothing. They always had something in their mouths they could spit, and where they spat didn't matter to them. They constantly complained that my fleas would jump across onto them; but they were never actually angry about it; they accepted as facts of life that fleas thrive in fur and that fleas are jumpers; they made their peace with it. When they were off duty, they would sometimes sit in a semicircle around me; hardly speaking, just grunting at each other; smoking their pipes as they lay stretched out on crates; slapping their thighs whenever I made the slightest movement; and now and then one of them would take a stick and scratch me where I liked it. If today I were invited to travel on that ship again I would certainly decline, but it's equally true that my memories of my time below decks are not all horrible.

The main effect of the calm I learnt among that circle of humans was to keep me from attempting any kind of escape. Looking back today, it seems as if I must have intuited at least that I had to find a way out if I wanted to live, but that that way out couldn't be found by escaping. I don't know any more whether escape was possible, but I imagine it was; for an ape, escape should always be possible. These days, my teeth are so weak I have to be careful just cracking a nut, but back then I should have managed eventually to bite through the lock. I didn't do it. What would I have gained? As soon as I'd stuck my head out of the cage, they'd have caught me again and locked me into somewhere even worse; or I would have crept in with the other animals, the giant constrictors, say, and sighed my last in their embrace; or I might even have managed to creep up onto the deck and throw myself overboard, where I would have bobbed around for a while before drowning. Acts of despair, all of them. I wasn't calculating in this human way, but under the influence of my surroundings I behaved as though I was.

As I say, I didn't calculate, but I quietly watched what was happening around me. I saw these humans come and go, always the same faces, the same movements; sometimes it seemed to me as if there were only one of them. This human or these humans could go where they wanted. A distant goal dawned on me. Nobody promised me that if I could become like them my cage would be opened. Promises aren't made on such seemingly impossible conditions. But if you succeed in fulfilling those conditions, those promises seem to retrospectively appear precisely where you previously searched for them in vain. Now, it has to be said that there was nothing very appealing about these humans in themselves. If I'd been a devotee of the freedom described earlier, I'm sure I would have preferred the ocean to the way out that I glimpsed in their dull faces. In any case, I watched them for a long time before I began to think of these things; in fact I think it was this mass of observations that pushed me in that direction.

It was so easy to imitate the humans. Spitting I managed after only a few days. After that we spat in each other's faces; the only difference was that I licked my face clean afterwards; they didn't. I could soon smoke a pipe like an old hand; if I then also tamped down the bowl with my thumb, the whole crew started cheering;

the only thing was that for a long time I couldn't grasp the difference between the pipe being full or empty.

What I had most trouble with was the rum bottle. Just the smell tormented me; I forced myself towards it with everything that I had, but weeks went by before I could overcome my own resistance. Strangely enough, the humans took this inner struggle more seriously than anything else about me. It's hard to distinguish between them in my memories, but there was one who came again and again, by himself or with the others, at all hours of day and night; he'd stand in front of me with a bottle and give me lessons. He didn't understand me and he wanted to solve the riddle of what I was. He slowly uncorked the bottle and looked at me to check whether I'd understood; I admit that I always watched him with greedy, savage attention; no teacher on earth could have found a pupil like me; after the bottle had been uncorked, he lifted it to his mouth; I follow with my eyes; he nods, he's pleased with me, and he puts the bottle to his lips; I'm delighted by incipient understanding and screech and scratch myself from head to toe; that makes him happy, he lifts the bottle and takes another swig; I'm impatient and desperate to imitate him, so I soil my cage, which he finds very satisfying; and then, holding out the bottle at arm's length before swinging it up to his mouth, and bending backwards exaggeratedly to help me understand, he empties it in one. Worn out by such a powerful sense of need, I can't follow what he's doing any more and just hang weakly from the bars, while he ends the theory lesson by rubbing his belly and grinning.

Only now do we move onto the practical lesson. Aren't I already too exhausted from the theory part? Yes, I'm completely drained. That's the way it goes. Nevertheless, I grab the proffered bottle as well as I can; uncork it, trembling; getting that to work makes me stronger; I lift the bottle, I'm already all but indistinguishable from the original; I put it to my mouth and—throw it away in disgust, in disgust, although it's empty and holds nothing more than the smell of what used to be inside; in disgust I throw the bottle on the floor. To the chagrin of my teacher, to my own greater chagrin, I remember—after I've thrown away the bottle—to rub my belly and give an exemplary grin.

All too often my lessons ran along these lines. And it's to the credit of my teacher that he was never angry with me; sometimes he did hold his burning pipe against my fur at some hard-to-reach spot until it began to smoulder, but he always extinguished it himself with a big, kindly hand; he wasn't angry with me, he understood that we were fighting on the same side against my simian nature and that my part of the struggle was harder.

So it was a victory for him as well as me when, one evening, in front of a big audience—it must have been some kind of celebration, a gramophone was playing, an officer was strolling around among the crew—on that evening, when I wasn't being watched, I reached for a bottle of rum accidentally left near my cage, opened it in textbook style, then, under the growing attention of the crowd, put it to my mouth and, without hesitating, without pulling my mouth away, like a first-class drinker, my eyes bulging, my Adam's apple bobbing, drank the whole thing dry; then threw the bottle away, not in desperation but as a flourish; admittedly forgot to rub my belly, but instead, because I couldn't stop myself, because I was urged on by something inside me, because my senses were reeling, I shouted "Hello!", breaking into human speech, making the leap into human society with that shout, and experiencing its echo—"Listen to that, he speaks!"—like a kiss pressed against my entire sweat-drenched body.

As I said earlier, I felt no longing to be like the humans; I imitated them because I was looking for a way out, and for no other reason. And even that victory didn't help me much. My voice immediately gave out again and only came back after months; my resistance to the rum bottle actually grew stronger; but my course had been set once and for all.

When I was handed over to my first trainer, in Hamburg, I soon recognized that there were two possibilities for me: the zoo or the variety shows. I didn't hesitate. I said to myself: strain every nerve to get into the variety shows; that's the way out; the zoo is just a different cage; if you end up in there, you're lost.

And I learnt, gentlemen. Oh, how you can learn when you have to; you learn because you want a way out; you learn ruthlessly. You hold the whip over your own head; you lacerate yourself at the slightest reluctance. My simian self, tumbling over itself in haste, rushed out of me so quickly that my first teacher became almost monkeyish in turn, soon having to give up the lessons and move into a psychiatric hospital. I'm glad to say he was quickly released again.

But I used up very many teachers, sometimes more than one teacher at once. As I became more confident in my abilities and the public began to follow my progress, when my future started to glitter, I took on my own teachers, had them set up in five connecting rooms, and learnt from all of them at once by leaping uninterruptedly from one room into the next.

What progress I made! Enlightenment broke into my awakening mind from every angle! I can't deny that it was a joy. But I can also admit that I never overestimated it, not even then and certainly not today. Through an effort that has never yet been paralleled anywhere in the world, I've reached the educational level of the average European. In itself, that's nothing at all, but it meant something insofar as it helped me get out of the cage and gave me this particular way out, the human way out. There's a wonderful idiom I love: to make yourself scarce. That's what I've done. I've made myself scarce. I had no other way open to me, since grand freedom wasn't on offer.

When I look back over my development and what I've achieved so far, I neither criticize myself nor am I content. Hands in my pockets, a bottle of wine on the table, I half sit, half lie in a rocking chair and look out of the window. If someone visits, I welcome them in politely. My manager sits in the front room; if I call, he comes in and listens to what I have to say. In the evenings, I almost always have a show, and my successes there probably won't be surpassed. When I come home late from a banquet, from a learned society, from some cosy get-together, I have a little half-trained chimp waiting for me, and I let her look after me in the simian style. I never see her during the day; she has the bewilderment of a trained animal in her eye; only I can see it and I can't bear to look at it.

Overall, I've certainly achieved what I wanted to achieve. I would never say that it hasn't been worth the effort. Nor am I looking for anyone's approval; I just want to spread what I've learnt. All I do is report on what I've experienced; even for you, gentlemen, members of the academy, all I've done is report.

HOMECOMING

I'VE COME BACK, come in through the gate, and I take a look around. It's my father's old farmyard. The puddle in the middle. Old, useless machinery, gathered into a heap, blocks the trapdoor into the cellar. The cat lurks on the railing. A torn piece of cloth, once wrapped around a pole in a game, lifts in the wind. I've arrived. Who'll be the one to greet me? Who's waiting behind the door to the kitchen? There's smoke rising out of the chimney, they're making coffee for their supper. Is it cosy, do you feel at home? I don't know, I'm not sure. It's my father's house, but each brick lies cold against the next, as if occupied with its own affairs, which I've partly forgotten, partly never knew. What use am I to them, even if I am my father's, the old farmer's, son. And I don't dare to knock at the kitchen door, I just listen from a distance, I listen standing at a distance, not so that I could be caught listening. And because I'm listening from a distance, I hear nothing, all I hear is a quiet clock chime, or I think I've heard it, chiming out of my childhood. What else is happening in the kitchen is a secret known only to those sitting inside it, who were here before me. The longer you hesitate outside the door, the more of a stranger you become. What would it be like if someone opened the door now and asked me a question. Wouldn't I seem like someone who wants to keep his secrets.

JACKALS AND ARABS

W E'D MADE CAMP at an oasis. The others were
asleep. An Arab, tall and white, came past me;
he'd been seeing to the camels and was heading for the
tents.

I threw myself down on the grass; I wanted to sleep,
but I couldn't; a jackal howled in the distance; I sat back
up again. And what had been far off was suddenly very
near. Jackals swarming all around me; eyes glowing a matt
gold before dulling again; slender bodies, their movements
as nimble and synchronized as if under threat of a whip.

One came forward from the back, pushed himself
under my arm, right up against me, as if he needed my
warmth, then stood in front of me so we were almost eye
to eye, and spoke: "I'm the oldest jackal anywhere round
here. And I'm glad I've lived long enough to welcome you.
I'd almost given up hope, because we've been waiting for
you almost since for ever; my mother waited for you, and
her mother, and all their mothers back to the mother of
all jackals. Believe me!"

"That's astonishing," I said, and forgot to light the wooden torch that was supposed to keep the jackals away with its smoke. "I'm astonished to hear that. It's only by chance that I've come here from the far north, and this is only a brief trip. What is it you want, jackals?"

And as if encouraged by what was maybe an over-friendly response, they drew their circle tighter around me; I could hear them panting quick and hot.

"We know," the oldest one went on, "that you come from the north, that's what our hopes are based on. Up there, you have a rationality that you'll never find among the Arabs. They're so cold and arrogant, you know, that you can never strike a spark of sense on them. They kill animals for food, and won't touch carrion."

"Not so loud," I said. "There are Arabs sleeping nearby."

"You really must be a foreigner," said the jackal. "Otherwise you would know that never in the history of the world has a jackal been afraid of an Arab. Be afraid of them? Isn't it bad enough that we have to live beside them?"

"Perhaps, perhaps," I said. "I wouldn't presume to judge things that are so alien to me; it seems to be a very old feud; it's probably in the blood, so it may well only end with bloodshed."

"You're very wise," said the old jackal, and they all panted even faster, their lungs racing even though they were standing still; a bitter stink streamed from their open muzzles and I sometimes had to clench my teeth to tolerate it. "You're very wise; what you say is in our ancient teachings. We'll take their blood and the feud will be over."

"Oh!" I said, more wildly than I wanted. "They'd defend themselves; they'd use guns to shoot you down in droves."

"You misunderstand us in the human way," he said, "even if you are from the far north. The Nile doesn't have enough water to wash us clean. Just the sight of their living bodies sends us running off for cleaner air, into the desert, that's why it's our home."

And all the jackals around me, who had been joined by many more from further away, put their heads down between their forelegs and scrubbed them with their paws; it was as if they were trying to hide their disgust, and it was so horrible that I would have liked to leap right over them, out of their circle, and flee.

"So what do you intend to do?" I asked, and tried to get up. I couldn't; two younger animals behind me had clamped their teeth into my jacket and shirt; I had no choice but to stay sitting. "They're holding your train," the old jackal explained seriously. "It's a mark of respect."

"Tell them to let go of me," I shouted, turning back and forth between the old jackal and the younger ones.

"Of course they will," said the old one, "if that's what you what. It'll take a little while, because, as is customary, they've bitten deep and will need a moment to unclamp their jaws. In the meantime, please hear our plea."

"Your behaviour hasn't made me especially well disposed to it," I said.

"Don't let our clumsiness count against us," he said, and now for the first time, he employed his voice's natural whine. "We're poor animals, all we have is our jaws; for everything we want to do, good or bad, it's our jaws or nothing."

"So what do you want?" I asked, only a little mollified.

"Sir," he cried, and all the jackals howled; I got a faraway sense that it was some kind of melody. "You must end the feud that divides the world in two. You are how the ancients described the one who would come to do that work. We must have peace from the Arabs; breathable air; our sight cleansed of their presence as far as every horizon; no more lamentation from the sheep the Arabs stab to death; all animals will die peacefully; we'll drink them dry without being disturbed and clean them all the way down to the bone. Cleanliness, cleanliness is all we want"—and now they were all crying, sobbing—"How can you stand it in this world, with your noble heart and sweet innards? Their white is dirty; their black is dirty; their beards are a horror; the look of their eyes makes you sick to the stomach; and if they raise their arms, a veritable hell opens up in their armpits. That's why, dear sir, oh, dearest sir, you must use your hands that can do anything, your hands that can do anything at all, to cut through their necks with these scissors!" He jerked his head and another jackal came forward; with one of his incisors he was holding a little rust-covered pair of sewing scissors.

"So finally the scissors—and that's enough!" shouted the Arab leading our caravan, who'd crept up to us from downwind and now cracked his enormous whip.

They all ran away at once, but then huddled together again at a distance, the many animals so close together and so still that they looked like they were in a narrow pen with a strange light flickering around them.

"So now you've seen and heard this performance as well, sir," said the Arab and laughed as happily as his people's reticence allowed.

"You know what the animals wanted?" I asked.

"Yes, sir," he said. "Everybody knows. That pair of scissors has been wandering the desert for as long as Arabs have existed, and it'll wander along behind us until the end of days. It's offered to every European who passes through so he can carry out their great work; each time, they think it's this European who's destined to do it. They're full of crazy hope, these animals; they're fools, real fools. That's why we love them; they're our dogs, lovelier than yours. Just watch: a camel died in the night and I've had it brought over."

Four bearers came and dropped the heavy cadaver in front of us. Hardly had they done so but the jackals lifted up their voices. As if pulled irresistibly forward by invisible tethers, each of them inched closer, hesitating, their bellies brushing the ground. They'd forgotten the Arabs, forgotten their hatred; the all-eclipsing presence of the pungent carcass bewitched them. One of them was already hanging on to the camel's neck and found its artery with the first bite. Each of the muscles in the jackal's body pulled and jerked in its place, like tiny, frenzied pumps trying eagerly but hopelessly to extinguish an enormous fire. Soon the other jackals had piled up on top of the cadaver and set about the same task.

Then the caravan leader slashed his whip hard across their backs. They lifted their heads, between delirium and unconsciousness; saw the Arabs standing in front of them; got the whip again across their muzzles; leapt backwards and ran a little way off. But the camel's blood already lay in steaming puddles, its body had been torn wide open in many places. They couldn't resist; they came back; the leader lifted his whip again; I touched his arm.

"You're right, sir," he said. "We'll leave them to their work; it's time for us to break camp. Anyway, you've seen them now. Wonderful animals, aren't they? And how they hate us!"

THE SILENCE OF
THE SIRENS

P ROOF THAT BASIC, even childish, methods can
sometimes save you:

To protect himself against the sirens, Odysseus stuffed
wax in his ears and had himself shackled to the mast. Of
course, every other sailor before him could have done the
same thing—except for those the Sirens had managed to
seduce from far away—but the whole world knew that
doing these things wouldn't help at all. The Sirens' song
could pierce anything, and the passion of those they
seduced would have burst through more than just some
chains and a mast. But that's not what Odysseus was
thinking of, even though he'd presumably heard about it.
He entrusted himself completely to a handful of wax and
his chains, and sailed towards the Sirens full of innocent
delight with his little trick.

But as it happens, the Sirens have a weapon even more
terrible than their singing, namely their silence. It may
never have happened, but it is at least conceivable that

someone could save himself from their singing; not so from their silence. The feeling of being able to overcome them with your own strength and the consequent reckless hubris would overwhelm any restraint on earth.

And in fact, when Odysseus came, those terrible singers didn't sing, whether because they believed that their opponent could only be reached by silence, or because the sight of the joy on Odysseus's face as he thought about his wax and his chains made them forget all about their singing.

Odysseus, however, if I can put it like this, didn't hear their silence; he believed that they were singing and that he alone was being protected from hearing them. At first, he saw their throats straining, their chests rising and falling, the tears in their eyes, their half-opened mouths, and thought that this was all part of the arias dying away unheard around him. But soon these things faded from his sight as he fixed his gaze into the distance; the Sirens all but melted away before his determination, and at the very moment when he was closest to them, his mind was already on other things.

But they—more beautiful than ever—stretched themselves and turned to follow him with their eyes, letting their gruesome hair blow in the wind and relaxing the grip of their claws on the rock. They didn't want to seduce him any more, all they wanted was to gaze on Odysseus's bright face for as long as they could.

If the Sirens had had a consciousness, that moment would have annihilated them. But as it was, they stayed there and Odysseus was the only one who ever escaped them.

A short postscript to this story has also been handed down. Odysseus, they say, was so cunning, he was such a sly fox, that even the goddess of fate couldn't see into his heart of hearts. It's possible—even though it goes beyond human understanding—that he actually did notice that the Sirens weren't singing, and put on this whole performance as a shield against them and the gods.

THE STOKER

WHEN THE SIXTEEN-YEAR-OLD Karl Rossmann, whose unfortunate parents had sent him to America because a servant girl had seduced him and had his child, sailed into the harbour at New York, he saw the Statue of Liberty, who'd already been visible for a while, suddenly bathed in a new light, as if the sunshine had grown stronger. The sword in her hand seemed only just to have been raised aloft, and the unchained breeze blew freely around her figure.

'It's so high!' he said to himself and, even though he'd momentarily forgotten all about disembarking, the swelling crowds of porters gradually pushed him up against the ship's railing.

A young man he'd got to know slightly on the crossing said as he went past, "Hey, don't you want to get off?"

"I'm ready," said Karl, laughing at him, and because he was a strong boy and feeling exuberant, he lifted his suitcase up to his shoulder. But as he looked past his acquaintance, who was swinging his stick and already starting to move off with the others, he realized with dismay that he'd forgotten his umbrella below decks. He quickly asked the acquaintance, who didn't look too happy about it, to do him a favour and watch his suitcase for a few minutes, then glanced around so that he'd be able to find this spot again, and hurried off. Unfortunately, when he got below he discovered that the most direct passageway had now been closed, probably something to do with the passengers disembarking, and he had to go searching down staircases that just led to more stairs, through constantly branching corridors, through an empty room with an abandoned writing desk, until, eventually, having only ever gone this way once or twice before, and then always as part of a big group, he was completely and utterly lost. Bewildered, meeting no one and hearing only the scrabbling of thousands of human feet above him, along with, far off, as if carried on a breeze, the last workings of the stopped engines, he began to bang on a little door that he'd come across as he wandered around.

"It's open!" someone shouted from inside, and Karl opened the door with a sincere sigh of relief. "Why are you banging on the door like a maniac?" asked an enormous man, barely glancing at Karl. From some overhead shaft, a murky light that had lost its lustre higher up the ship fell into the wretched cabin, in which a bed, a cupboard, a chair and the man stood pressed against each other as if in storage. "I've lost my bearings," said Karl. "I didn't really notice on the crossing, but it's such a big ship."

"You're right there," the man said with some pride, and carried on tinkering with the lock on a small suitcase, which he kept shutting with both hands so he could listen to it clicking into place. "But come on in," said the man, "Surely you're not just going to stand out there!"

"I'm not disturbing you?" asked Karl.

"Come off it, how would you be disturbing me?"

"Are you German?" Karl tried to reassure himself, having heard a lot about the dangers that awaited new arrivals in America, especially from Irishmen.

"I am, I am," said the man. Karl still hesitated. The man abruptly grabbed the door handle and, closing it rapidly, pulled Karl into the room with him. "I hate it when people look in at me from the corridor," said the man, who'd gone back to working on his suitcase. "Everybody just walks past and looks inside, I can't put up with that."

"But the corridor's completely empty," said Karl, who was squashed uncomfortably against the bedpost.

"It is now," said the man.

'But now is what we're talking about,' thought Karl, 'This man's hard to have a conversation with.'

"Lie on the bed, you'll have more space," said the man. Karl squirmed over as well as he could and laughed out loud at his first failed attempt to swing himself into it. But hardly was he in the bed than he cried, "Oh God, I've totally forgotten my suitcase!"

"Where is it?"

"Up on the deck, someone I met is keeping an eye on it. Oh, what's his name again?" And he pulled a calling card out of the secret pocket his mother had sewn into the lining of his coat for the journey. "Butterbaum. Franz Butterbaum."

"Do you really need the things in your suitcase?"

"Of course."

"Then why did you give it to a stranger?"

"I forgot my umbrella below decks and came down to fetch it, but didn't want to lug the suitcase around with me. And then I got lost."

"You're by yourself? Not with anyone?"

"Yes, by myself." 'Maybe I should stick with this man,' went through Karl's head, 'Where could I quickly find a better friend?'

"And now you've lost the suitcase too. To say nothing of the umbrella." The man sat down on the chair as if Karl's affairs had become more interesting.

"I'm sure the suitcase is still there."

"Be as sure as you like," said the man, and had a good scratch at his short, dark, thick hair, "but on a ship the way people behave changes with each port. In Hamburg maybe your Butterbaum really would have watched your suitcase, here it's most likely they've both already vanished."

"But then I've got to go up and look for it," said Karl, glancing around for how to clamber back out.

"Just stay," said the man, and thrust his hand against Karl's chest, almost roughly, pushing him back onto the bed.

"But why?" asked Karl angrily.

"Because there's no point," said the man. "In a little while I'll be going too, then we can go together. Either the suitcase has been stolen, in which case it can't be helped, or your Butterbaum left it standing there, in which case it'll be all the easier to find once the ship's empty. The same goes for your umbrella."

"Do you know your way around the ship?" asked Karl distrustfully, and it seemed to him that this generally convincing idea, that it would be easiest to find his things when the ship was empty, had a hidden catch.

"I'm one of the ship's stokers," said the man.

"You're a stoker!" cried Karl happily, as though that surpassed all his expectations, and, propping himself up on his elbows, he took a closer look at the man. He said, "Just next to the cabin where I was sleeping, near the Slovak, there was a hatch where you could see into the engine room."

"Yes, that's where I was working," said the stoker.

"I've always been interested in machinery," said Karl, following his own train of thought, "and I would definitely have become an engineer if I hadn't had to go to America."

"Why did you have to go?"

"Never mind," said Karl, and waved the whole story away. While doing so he smiled at the stoker, as if asking him to be lenient about this thing Karl hadn't admitted.

"There will have been a reason," said the stoker, and it wasn't clear whether he wanted to hear the story or deflect it.

"Now I suppose I could be a stoker too," said Karl, "My parents don't care at all any more about what I end up doing."

"My job's coming up," said the stoker, then coolly put his hands in his pockets and slung his legs, clad in wrinkled, leathery, iron-grey trousers, onto the bed to stretch them out. Karl had to shift closer against the wall.

"You're leaving the ship?"

"Absolutely, we're going ashore today."

"Why? Don't you like it?"

"Well, it's a question of circumstances, it's not always about whether you like it or not. But as it happens, you're right, I don't like it. You're probably not seriously thinking about becoming a stoker, but that's exactly the state of mind in which you're most likely to become one. I strongly advise you against it. If you wanted to study when you were in Europe, why don't you want to study here? The American universities are so much better than the European ones."

"You might be right," said Karl, "but I've hardly got enough money for studying. I did read about someone who worked in a shop during the day and studied at night until he became a doctor and I think the mayor of a town, but you need a huge amount of stamina for that, don't you? I'm worried I don't have it. Also I wasn't an especially good pupil; having to leave school wasn't something I was particularly sad about. And the schools here are maybe even stricter. I can barely speak English at all. And people here are so much against foreigners, I think."

"Have you noticed that already? Well, that's all right. Then you're the man for me. Look here, we're on a German ship, aren't we, it belongs to the Hamburg–America Line, why aren't we all Germans? Why is the chief engineer a Romanian? He's called Schubal. It's unbelievable. And this lousy bastard orders us Germans around on a German ship! Don't think,"—he ran out of breath and flapped his hands in the air—"that I'm complaining just for the sake of complaining. I know you don't have any influence and you're just a poor young lad yourself. But it's too much!" And he banged his fist several times on the table, watching it as he did so. "I've already served on so many ships"—he listed twenty names as if they were a single word, which Karl couldn't follow— "and I've distinguished myself on them, been praised, been a worker the captains liked, I even stayed on the same merchant clipper for *years*"—he lifted himself up as if this were the high point of his life—"and here on this tub, where they lead you around by the nose, where you don't need any brains, here I'm not worth anything, here I'm always in Schubal's way, I'm a slacker, I deserve to be thrown out and I only get my pay out of pity. Does that make sense to you? It doesn't to me."

"You can't stand for that," said Karl, getting worked up. He felt so at home here on the stoker's bed that he'd almost forgotten he was on the uncertain ground of a ship moored to the coast of an unknown continent. "Have you been to see the captain? Have you asked him for your rights?"

"Oh, go away, why don't you leave? I don't want you here. You don't listen to what I'm saying and then you give me advice. How am I supposed to go to the captain!" The stoker wearily sat back down and put his face in his hands.

'I've got no better advice to give him,' Karl said to himself. And he was starting to think he'd be better off going to find his suitcase than staying down here to give advice that wasn't wanted. When his father handed him the suitcase to keep for ever, he'd asked, as a joke, "How long will you have this for?" and now that expensive suitcase was perhaps already lost in earnest. Karl's only consolation was that there was no way his father could ever find out about the situation he was in, even if he did try to make enquiries. That Karl had come as far as New York was all the shipping line would be able to tell him. It pained Karl that he hadn't even really used some of the things in the suitcase, even though, for example, he'd needed to change his shirt for a while now. He'd scrimped in the wrong place there; at the start of his American career, just when he most needed to present himself in clean clothes, he'd have to turn up in a dirty shirt. If it hadn't been for that, the loss of the suitcase wouldn't have been so bad, because the suit he was wearing was actually better than the one in the case, which was really just an emergency suit that his mother had quickly darned right before he left. He also remembered that there'd been a piece of Verona salami in there, which his mother had packed as a treat and which he'd eaten very little of, because he'd had hardly any appetite at all on the crossing and the soup they'd doled out in steerage had been more than enough for him. He would have liked to have the salami handy so he could give it to the stoker as a present. People like that are easily won over if you slip them something small; Karl had learnt that from his father, who gave out cigars and so won over all the low-ranking staff he dealt with in his work. The only thing Karl had left to give away was his money, and since it looked like he'd already lost his suitcase, he wanted to leave that where it was for the time being. His thoughts kept coming back to the suitcase, and now he simply could not understand why he'd watched his suitcase so closely on the crossing that it had almost ruined his sleep, only to then let that same suitcase be so easily taken away from him. He thought of the five nights in which he'd been absolutely convinced that a small Slovak lying five bunks to his left had his sights on his suitcase. This Slovak was just waiting for the moment when Karl, overcome by fatigue, finally nodded off for a minute, so that he could pull the suitcase towards himself using a long pole which he played and practised with from morning till night. By day the Slovak looked innocent enough, but as soon as night fell, he started getting up from time to time and glancing sadly across at Karl's suitcase. Karl could see that very clearly, because here and there someone suffering the emigrant's restlessness would always strike a little light, despite that being against the on-board regulations, and try to decipher the incomprehensible prospectuses of migration agencies. If one of those lights was nearby, Karl could doze a little, but if it was far off, or if the room was dark, then he had to keep his eyes open. The effort had worn him out and now it had perhaps all been for nothing. That Butterbaum—if Karl ever got hold of him again!

At that moment, the former total quiet outside was interrupted by a far-off pattering, as if of children's feet; it came nearer, grew louder, and then it became the measured tread of men. They were obviously going single file along the narrow passageway and you could hear a light jingling like that of weapons. Karl, who'd been close to stretching himself out on the bed and falling into a sleep released from all worries about suitcases and Slovaks, started upright and jabbed the stoker to make him pay attention, because the head of the column seemed to have just reached the door. "That's the ship's band," said the stoker, "They've been playing on deck and now they're going to pack up their things. That means it's all over and we can go. Come on!" He took Karl by the hand, then, at the last second, pulled a framed picture of the Madonna off the wall and stuffed it into his breast pocket, grabbed his suitcase and hurried Karl out of the cabin.

"Now I'm going to go up to the office and give those gentlemen a piece of my mind. There aren't any passengers around any more, no need to keep quiet for their sake." The stoker repeated this several times in various formulations, and, in passing, tried to use the side of his foot to crush a rat that was crossing the passageway, but succeeded only in kicking it faster into the hole that it reached just in time. He moved slowly in general, and although he had long legs, they were too heavy.

They went through a part of the kitchens where several girls in dirty aprons—they splattered them on purpose—were washing dishes in big tubs. The stoker called over one of the girls, Lina, put his arm around her waist and led her along for a few steps while she pressed herself coquettishly against him. "It's cashing-out time, do you want to come?" he asked.

"Why should I bother, you can just bring me the money here," she answered, then slipped out from under his arm and ran away. "Where did you dig up that beautiful boy?" she called after them, but didn't stop for an answer. The other girls, who'd paused their work to listen, all laughed.

Karl and the stoker continued on and reached a door topped with a small portico held up by little golden caryatids. By the standard of ship's furnishings, it looked downright lavish. Karl realized that he'd never been to this section, which had probably been reserved for first- and second-class passengers during the crossing, whereas now the dividing doors had been taken out for the ship's deep clean. They'd already come across men carrying brooms over their shoulders, who'd said hello to the stoker. Karl was astonished by how busy it was; down in steerage he hadn't seen much of what was going on. There were even electrical cables running along the corridors and a tinny bell kept ringing.

The stoker knocked respectfully on the door and, when someone shouted "Enter," he gestured at Karl not to be afraid and to come in. Karl did go inside, but stayed close to the door. Out of the room's three windows he could see the waves of the open sea, and as he watched their cheerful movement, his heart thudded as if he hadn't just been looking at the sea nonstop for five long days. Huge ships crossed one another's paths, so heavy that they shifted only slightly with the force of the waves. If you narrowed your eyes, it looked as if these ships were swaying under their own weight. On their masts they flew long, narrow flags, blown taut by their speed but still wriggling from side to side. Gun salutes rang out, presumably from warships, and the long barrels of one passing quite close by, shining brightly as the sun struck its steel cladding, were rocked back and forth by the ship's steady, smooth but not quite perfectly horizontal motion. The smaller boats and launches could only be seen in the distance, at least when standing by the door, but there were swarms of them running in through the gaps between the big ships. Behind all this stood New York, watching Karl through its skyscrapers' hundred thousand windows. Yes, in this room you knew where you were.

At a round table sat three men, one a ship's officer in his blue jacket, the two others officials from the port authority in black American uniforms. Stacked high on the table in front of them were all sorts of documents, which the officer skimmed over with a pen in his hand, then passed to the two others, who read or copied out certain sections and put them in their briefcases, pausing only when one of them, who kept making a clicking noise with his teeth, dictated something for his colleague's report.

Sitting at a desk by the window, with his back to the door, sat a diminutive man working through a row of heavy ledgers lined up at his eye level on a strong shelf. Next to him was an open, empty-looking cash box.

The second window was unobstructed and gave the best view. Near the third, however, stood two more gentlemen having a murmured conversation. One, wearing a naval uniform and toying with the hilt of his sword, was leaning against the window frame. The man he was talking to was facing the window, and now and then his movements revealed part of a row of decorations on the first man's chest. He was in civilian clothes and carried a thin bamboo cane, which, because his hands were on his hips, stuck out like a sword of his own.

Karl didn't have much time to take all this in because a steward came up to them and, giving the stoker a look that plainly said he didn't belong there, asked what he wanted. The stoker answered, as quietly as he'd been asked, that he would like to speak to the chief purser. The steward, for his part, rejected this request with a gesture, but nonetheless walked softly across to the man with the ledgers, making a wide detour around the table. The purser—you could see it clearly—literally stiffened at what the steward said to him, but eventually turned towards the stoker and sternly waved his hand to dismiss him, and then dismissed the steward, too, for good measure. At that, the steward came back to the stoker and, as if confiding something to him, said, "Leave this room at once!"

Upon receiving this response, the stoker looked down at Karl as if Karl were the stoker's heart and he were silently lamenting his sorrows to it. Without a second thought, Karl set off and marched straight across the room, even lightly brushing the officer's chair as he passed; the steward went after him, leaning forward with his arms held out ready to grab him, as if he were chasing a bug, but Karl was first to the purser's table and he held on to it in case the steward tried to pull him away.

Of course the whole room suddenly got very lively. The officer at the table jumped to his feet, the men from the port authority were calm but alert, the two gentlemen at the window stepped closer together, while the steward retreated, believing that anywhere the higher-ups showed an interest was somewhere he was out of place. The stoker, still by the door, waited nervously for his help to be called upon. The chief purser finally swung his chair around to the right.

Karl rummaged in his secret pocket, which he had no hesitation in revealing to these people, fished out his passport and laid it open on the table without any other introduction. The chief purser seemed to consider this passport irrelevant and flicked it aside with his fingers, at which Karl, as if this formality had been correctly taken care of, put it back in his pocket.

"I have to say," he then began, "that in my opinion this stoker has been unjustly treated. There's a certain

Schubal who keeps doing him down. He's already served on very many ships, all of which he can name for you, to the complete satisfaction of their captains, he's hard-working, takes his job seriously, and it really doesn't make any sense that, on this one ship, where what's required isn't especially difficult, not like it is on a merchant clipper, for example, he wouldn't be up to the mark. It can therefore only be slander that's preventing him from getting ahead and robbing him of the recognition he deserves, and which he would certainly otherwise be getting. I'm only giving the general outline here, the specific complaints he'll present to you himself." Karl had directed this speech to everyone in the room, because they were already listening and because it seemed far more likely that there would be one fair-minded man among the group than that that man would happen to be the chief purser. Cunningly, Karl had omitted that he'd known the stoker for such a short time. And he would actually have spoken much better if he hadn't been thrown off by the red face of the gentleman with the bamboo cane, which he could see properly from his new vantage point.

"It's all true, every word," said the stoker before anyone had asked him, indeed before anyone had even looked at him. This over-hastiness would have been a big mistake had the gentleman with the decorations, who Karl now realized was the captain, not already made the decision to listen to the stoker. He reached out his hand and told the stoker, "Come over here!" with a voice so hard you could have hit it with a hammer. Now everything depended on the impression the stoker made; Karl didn't have any doubts about the rightness of his cause.

Luckily, in this moment it turned out that the stoker was a man of the world. With exemplary calm, he neatly fished a little bundle of papers and a notebook out of his suitcase and, as if it were the obvious thing to do, simply bypassed the chief purser and took his papers straight to the captain, for whom he spread his evidence out on the window sill. The chief purser had no choice but to go over there himself. "The man is a well-known troublemaker," he said in explanation, "He spends more time at the cash desk than in the engine room. He's driven Schubal, that quiet soul, to the brink of desperation. Now listen here!" he turned to the stoker, "don't you think you've finally taken this pushiness of yours too far? How many times have you already been thrown out by the cashiers, just as you and your completely and utterly unwarranted demands entirely deserve! How many times have you come running from there to this office! How often have you already been told, quite rightly, that Schubal is your direct superior and that it's him you have to sort these things out with! And now you've got so shameless that you come barging in when the captain's present and bother him with this, and you're not even embarrassed about bringing along this boy, who I've never seen on the ship before, to trot out these ridiculous allegations for you!"

Karl had to keep himself from lunging forward. But the captain was already there, saying, "Let's hear what the man has to say. It's true that Schubal has recently been getting a bit too independent for my liking—which isn't to say anything in your favour." The latter was directed at the stoker, but it was natural that the captain couldn't take up his case just like that, and everything seemed to be on the right track. The stoker began his explanation and even managed to give Schubal the title "Mr". How happy Karl was, standing by the chief purser's abandoned desk, where he kept pressing down a parcel scale with his fingers, out of sheer delight. — Mr Schubal is unfair! Mr Schubal gives preferential treatment to foreigners! Mr Schubal ejected the stoker from the engine room and sent him to scrub the toilet, which was certainly not his job! — At one point doubt was even cast on Mr Schubal's work ethic, which was apparently discussed rather more than it really existed. At that, Karl stared at the captain with all his might, candidly, as though they were colleagues, so that he wouldn't let himself be unfavourably influenced by the stoker's slightly clumsy way of expressing himself. Nevertheless, for all the stoker talked, he didn't actually bring up anything concrete, and although the captain still looked straight at him, his face set with determination to hear him out this time, the other men started to get impatient and the stoker's voice lost its hold on the room's attention, which was not a good sign. The first was the gentleman in civilian clothes who began to toy with his bamboo cane, tapping it, albeit quietly, on the parquet floor. The others began to glance around the room and the two officials from the port authority, who were obviously pressed for time, took up their files and started looking through them again, if still a bit absent-mindedly; the ship's officer shifted his chair closer to them, and the chief purser, who thought he'd won the day, heaved a deep and ironic sigh. Only the steward seemed unaffected by the air of distraction that was setting in among the others, because he sympathized with the plight of a poor man put in front of the powerful, and he nodded seriously at Karl as if trying to assure him of something.

Meanwhile, the life of the harbour went on outside the window: a flat cargo barge carrying a mountain of barrels, which must have been ingeniously stacked not to roll off, went by and plunged the room into shadow; small motor launches, which Karl could now have got a good look at if he'd had a moment, swooshed past in dead straight lines, twitching with the hands of the men standing upright at the helms; strange floating objects kept popping up out of the unsettled waters, but they were swamped again at once and sank out of Karl's astonished sight; boats belonging to the ocean liners were rowed ashore by toiling sailors, each stuffed with passengers who quietly and expectantly sat where they'd been told to, even though a few couldn't resist turning their heads from side to side to see the changing backdrop. It was motion without end, a restlessness transferred from the restless deep to these helpless people and their works!

The whole situation urged speed, clarity, the most precise description, but what did the stoker do? He talked himself up into a sweat, his hands trembled so much he couldn't hold the papers on the window sill; he thought of endless complaints to make about Schubal and in his opinion any one of them should have been enough to bury him for good, but what he managed to present to the captain was just a sad mishmash of all of them. The man with the bamboo cane had already started whistling quietly and looking at the ceiling, the men from the port authority had drawn the ship's officer over to their table and showed no sign of releasing him again, the chief purser was visibly holding himself back from butting in only because the captain had stayed so calm, and the steward was waiting attentively for the order that the captain must soon give about what to do with the stoker.

Karl couldn't stand idly by any longer. He went slowly over to the group, and as he went he thought quickly about the cleverest way he could get a grip on what was happening. The time was ripe: only a little more of this and he and the stoker would both be thrown out of the office. The captain might be a good man and might also, as it seemed to Karl, have some particular reason for presenting himself as a fair commander, but at the end of the day he wasn't an instrument you could play however you wanted—and that was exactly how the stoker was trying to handle him, albeit out of sincere and boundless indignation.

Karl said to the stoker: "You've got to explain it more simply, more clearly; the captain can't take it seriously, the way you're explaining it. Do you think the captain knows the surname of every engineer and errand boy, or their Christian names, so that you can just refer to them like that and he'll know who you're talking about? You've got to arrange your complaints, say the most important thing first, then the other things in descending order, and it might turn out that most of them you don't even have to mention. You've always explained it so clearly to me!" If you can steal suitcases in America, you can also tell a little white lie here and there, he thought apologetically.

If only it had helped! Wasn't it already too late? The stoker broke off as soon as he heard Karl's familiar voice, but his eyes were glazed with the tears of wounded male pride, of dreadful memories, of an extreme predicament, and he couldn't even properly make out Karl's face any more. How could he now—Karl silently understood this as he stood in front of the silent man—how could he now suddenly change his whole manner of speech, especially when it must seem to him that he'd already put forward all there was to say, without anything to show for it, while at the same time, it also seemed that he hadn't really said anything yet and couldn't expect these gentlemen to keep on listening to the rest of the story. And in this moment, here comes Karl, his only supporter, trying to give him some good advice, but instead only showing him that all, truly all, is lost.

'If only I'd come quicker instead of looking out of the window,' Karl said to himself, then bowed his face away from the stoker and clapped his hands against the seams of his trousers as a sign that every hope was at an end.

But the stoker misunderstood, somehow getting the idea that Karl was secretly criticizing him, and, hoping to win him round, he—on top of everything—started to quarrel with Karl. He did so at a point when the men at the round table had long since become resentful of the unnecessary noise disturbing their important work, when the chief purser was beginning to find the captain's patience incomprehensible and was on the brink of erupting, when the steward had reverted to being entirely his bosses' man and was weighing up the stoker with a wild look in his eye, and when the gentleman with the bamboo cane, to whom the captain occasionally sent a friendly glance and who was by now totally indifferent to the stoker, even disgusted by him, took out a small notebook and, evidently preoccupied with something else entirely, let his attention wander back and forth between the notebook and Karl.

"I know, I know," said Karl, who was finding it difficult to defend himself against the tirade that the stoker had now directed at him, but nevertheless still kept up an amiable smile for him. "You're quite right, absolutely, I never doubted it." He would have liked to grab the stoker's gesticulating hands, for fear of being struck, but would have liked even more to push him into a corner and whisper a few quiet, comforting words that no one else would have needed to hear. But the stoker was totally beside himself. Karl began to take some solace from the thought that, if need be, the stoker would be able to subdue all seven men present with the strength of his despair. On the desk, however, there was a raised section with far too many buttons, all connected to the electrical system; simply pressing a hand down on it would have roused the whole ship and filled its corridors with people hostile to them.

At that moment, the seemingly indifferent man with the bamboo cane approached Karl and asked, not loudly, but in a voice distinct despite all the stoker's yelling, "What's your name?" At the same time, as if someone had been waiting for the man to speak, there was a knocking at the door. The steward looked to the captain, who nodded. The steward went to the door and opened it. Outside in an old military-style coat stood a man of middling build who, judging by his appearance, didn't seem very well suited to working with machines, yet was in fact Schubal. If Karl hadn't realized that from the way everyone looked at him, betraying a certain satisfaction that even the captain wasn't above, he couldn't have missed, to his shock, that the stoker tensed his arms and balled his fists as if these fists were the most important thing about him, for which he would have sacrificed whatever he had in life. All his strength, even what kept him on his feet, had gone there.

And so that was the enemy, free and fresh in his smart clothes, with a book of accounts under his arm, probably the stoker's hours and pay, and he looked each of them in the eye in turn, not afraid to let them see that he was gauging their mood. All seven were already on his side, because although the captain had had certain reservations about him, or pretended to have them after feeling nettled by the stoker, Schubal now seemed above even the smallest criticism. You couldn't be strict enough with a man like the stoker, and if Schubal had done anything wrong, it was that he'd failed to break the stoker's wilfulness before he could dare present himself in front of the captain.

You might have assumed that a confrontation between the stoker and Schubal before this group of people would have the same effect as one before a higher court, and that even if Schubal was good at disguising his real character, he wouldn't be able to keep it up till the end. A brief flash of malice would be enough of a demonstration for these men, and Karl wanted to make sure it happened. He'd been able to pick up a little about the acumen, weaknesses and temper of each of the men, and, seen from that perspective, the time he'd spent here had not been wasted. If only the stoker would make a better impression, but he seemed completely unable to stand up for himself. If you'd held Schubal within his reach, the stoker would presumably have managed to bash in his hated skull with his fists. But just to take a few steps over to Schubal would have been beyond him. Why hadn't Karl predicted what was so easily predictable, namely that Schubal would eventually have to appear, either under his own impetus or called in by the captain. Why hadn't Karl and the stoker worked out a precise plan of attack on the way here rather than walking in hopelessly unprepared simply because the door was in front of them? Was the stoker even still capable of speech, of saying yes and no when required to in the impending cross-examination, which, at this rate, they would be lucky even to get to? He was standing there with his legs apart, his knees unsteady, his head lifted slightly, with the air going in and out of his mouth as if he had no lungs left to absorb it.

Karl, meanwhile, felt stronger and more lucid than he perhaps ever had back home. If his parents could only see him now, in a foreign country, championing a just cause in front of distinguished persons, and although he hadn't won yet, he was ready to make a final push. Would that change their opinion of him? Would they sit him down between them and praise him? Look him once, just once, in the eyes that gazed at them with such devotion? What dubious questions and what an inopportune moment to start asking them!

"I've come because I believe that the stoker is accusing me of some kind of dishonesty. A girl from the kitchens told me she'd seen him on his way here. Captain, gentlemen, I'm ready to disprove any allegation by referring to my records and, if necessary, with the testimony of impartial and independent witnesses, who are waiting outside the door." Thus spoke Schubal. It was the clear speech of a mature man, and from the change in the expression of his listeners you might have thought this was the first time in a long time they'd heard a human voice. They certainly didn't notice that even this fine speech was riddled with holes. Why was the first specific charge that occurred to him "dishonesty"? Perhaps the stoker's allegations should have started there rather than with his national prejudices? A girl from the kitchen had seen the stoker on the way to the office and Schubal had understood at once what was going on? Wasn't it guilt that sharpened his powers of understanding? And on top of that he'd immediately brought along a gang of witnesses, whom he had the nerve to call impartial and independent? It was a racket, one big racket! And these gentlemen were letting it go on and clearly even considered this the right way to behave? Why had Schubal let so much time pass between getting the message from the girl in the kitchens and showing himself here? Surely for no other reason than to let the stoker wear everybody out until it fogged their judgment, which Schubal had good reason to be afraid of. Hadn't Schubal, who must have been standing outside the door for a long time already, only knocked when that gentleman had asked an unrelated question, which suggested that the stoker was finished?

It was all crystal clear and Schubal was giving himself away despite everything, but these gentlemen still needed it put to them even more straightforwardly. They needed to be shaken up. 'Karl,' he thought, 'it's time to act, before the witnesses come in and swamp the conversation.'

But right at that moment, the captain waved Schubal away, and he—since his affairs seemed to have been postponed for a little while—stepped aside and began a hushed conversation with the steward, who'd joined him at once, a conversation with no shortage of sidelong glances at the stoker and Karl, nor of emphatic hand gestures. Schubal looked to be preparing his next big speech.

"Didn't you want to ask this young man something, Mr Jakob?" said the captain to the man with the bamboo cane over the general hush.

"Indeed," he said, thanking the captain for this courtesy with a slight bow. And then he asked Karl again, "What's your name?"

Karl, who believed it was in the interest of their cause to dispense with this interlude and his stubborn questioner as quickly as possible, answered curtly, breaking his habit of introducing himself by presenting his passport, which he would anyway first have had to find: "Karl Rossmann."

"But," said the man the captain had called Jakob, immediately taking a step back, smiling almost in disbelief. The captain, the chief purser, the ship's officer, even the steward also appeared to be inexplicably astonished by Karl's name. Only the men from the port authority and Schubal didn't react.

"But," Mr Jakob repeated, coming over to Karl on stiff legs, "that means I'm your Uncle Jakob and you're my dear nephew. I suspected it from the very start!" he said to the captain, before putting his arms around Karl and kissing him, while Karl silently let it happen.

"What's your name?" Karl asked after being released, speaking very politely but not feeling at all moved, and trying to predict what the consequences of this new development might be for the stoker. For the time being, there seemed no reason to believe that Schubal would be able to turn it to his advantage.

"Try to understand how lucky you are, young man," said the captain, who thought that Karl's question had wounded the dignity of Mr Jakob, who'd gone over to the window, evidently so that the others wouldn't see the emotion on his face, which he was dabbing with a handkerchief. "The man who's just told you he's your uncle is Senator Edward Jakob. From now on, a glittering career awaits you, presumably quite in contrast with what you'd been expecting. Try to grasp that as well as you can right now, and get a hold of yourself!"

"I really do have an Uncle Jakob in America," said Karl to the captain, "but if I've understood correctly, Jakob is the senator's surname."

"That's right," the captain said, and waited for him to go on.

"Well, my Uncle Jakob, who's my mother's brother, it's only his Christian name that's Jakob, and his surname must obviously be the same as my mother's, whose maiden name is Bendelmayer."

"Gentlemen!" cried the senator, coming back very cheerfully from his restorative break by the window, and referring to what Karl had just explained. All of them, with the exception of the port officials, burst out laughing, some seeming genuinely touched, others more inscrutably.

'What I said wasn't that ridiculous,' Karl thought to himself.

"Gentlemen," repeated the senator, "without your meaning to, or my meaning you to, you are witnessing a little family scene, and I feel I owe you some explanation for it, since, I believe, only the captain"—this mention elicited an exchange of bows—"knows the full story."

'Now I've really got to pay attention to every word,' Karl said to himself and, looking over his shoulder, he was happy to see that the figure of the stoker was coming back to life.

"For all the long years of my American sojourn—the word sojourn isn't actually quite right for someone who's an American citizen, as I am with every part of my soul—but for all these long years I've been living entirely estranged from my European family, for reasons that are firstly not relevant here, and secondly would be too distressing to relate. In fact, I've already begun to dread the time when I will have to explain it to my dear nephew, a task that will make it impossible not to say some frank words about his parents and their friends."

'He's my uncle, no doubt about it,' Karl said to himself, and listened. 'He must have just changed his name.'

"My dear nephew's parents have—let's call this thing what it is—simply got rid of him, the way you put a cat outside when it annoys you. I certainly don't want to play down what my nephew did to elicit that punishment, but his misdemeanour is such that just describing it excuses him."

'I'd like to hear that,' thought Karl, 'but I don't want him to tell it to everyone. And aside from that, he can't know anything about it. How could he?'

"What happened," continued his uncle, leaning his weight onto the bamboo cane and rocking back and forth a little, which removed some of the unnecessary solemnity that this subject would otherwise have certainly taken on, "what happened is that he was seduced by a serving maid, Johanna Brummer, a woman of around thirty-five. It's not my intention to embarrass my nephew with the word 'seduce', but it's hard to find another that fits."

Karl, who had moved to stand quite close to his uncle, turned around at that moment to read the effect of the story on the faces of those present. Nobody laughed, all of them listened patiently and seriously. After all, you don't laugh about the nephew of a senator just like that. If anything, you would have thought that the stoker was smiling very faintly at Karl, which was both gratifying as a new sign of life and excusable in him because, when they'd been together in his cabin, Karl had tried to keep secret this thing that was now being made so public.

"Then this Brummer," his uncle continued, "had a child by my nephew, a healthy boy, baptized with the name Jakob, doubtless as a reference to myself, who must have made a strong impression on the girl in what I'm sure were merely passing mentions by my nephew. And a good thing too, I say. Because since his parents wanted to avoid maintenance payments or whatever other aspects of the scandal would have touched them—I must emphasize that I'm not familiar with either the laws over there or his parents' general circumstances—but since they wanted to avoid maintenance payments and a scandal, they had their son, my dear nephew, shipped off to America with an irresponsible lack of material provisions, as you can see, meaning that, had it not been for one of the miracles that can apparently still happen in America, the boy would have immediately met his death in some New York back alley, except that the serving girl wrote me a letter which, after many detours, arrived in my possession yesterday, telling me the whole story as well as providing a description of my nephew and—very sensibly—the name of this ship. If I wanted to entertain you, gentlemen, I could just read out some choice passages from that letter"—he pulled two enormous, closely handwritten sheets of paper from his pocket and waved them around. "I've no doubt you would find it affecting, since it's written with a certain amount of quite crude but well-meaning guile, and with a great deal of love for the father of her child. But it's neither my purpose to entertain you more than is necessary to explain what you're witnessing, nor, in this moment of welcome, to run the risk of injuring any feelings that my nephew may still have for her, especially as, if he likes, he can read the letter for his own information in the privacy of the room that's already been prepared for him."

Karl, however, didn't have any feelings for that girl. Amid the confusion of an ever more distant past, she was sitting in her kitchen with one elbow propped on the dresser. She looked at him when he came into the kitchen now and then to fetch a glass of water for his father or to run an errand for his mother. Sometimes she was writing a letter from her cramped position next to the dresser, and would draw her inspiration from Karl's face. Sometimes she covered her eyes with one hand and then nothing he said could reach her. Sometimes she got onto her knees in her narrow little room next to the kitchen and prayed to a wooden cross; Karl would watch her shyly through the crack of the door as he went in and out. Sometimes she raced around the kitchen and, if Karl got in her way, she'd flinch backwards, cackling like a witch. Sometimes she closed the door to the kitchen after Karl had come in and held on to the handle until he asked to be let out. Sometimes she brought him things that he didn't even want and silently pressed them into his hands. But once she said "Karl" and, amid sighs and grimaces, led him—still astonished by being addressed in this unexpected way—to her room, and locked the door. She flung her arms around his neck tight enough to choke him and, although she asked him to undress her, she actually undressed him and laid him on her bed as though from now on she would keep him all to herself and caress and care for him until the end of the world. "Karl, oh my Karl!" she cried as if she'd just seen him and was reassuring herself that she had him, while he couldn't see a thing and felt ill at ease among the mass of warm bedclothes that she seemed to have heaped up for his sake. Then she lay down next to him and wanted to hear some kind of secrets, but he couldn't think of anything and she got cross, whether joking or for real, shook him, listened to his heart, offered her breast for him to listen to, pressed her naked stomach against his body, sent her hand searching between his legs so horribly that Karl shook his head and neck free of the pillows, then thrust her stomach against him several times—it seemed as if she'd become a part of him and perhaps for that reason he was gripped by a terrible helplessness. In tears, and after many tender goodnights on her part, he'd finally got back to his own bed. That was all it had been and somehow his uncle was turning it into this whole big story. And it seemed the cook had been thinking of him and had written to tell his uncle he was coming. That was very good of her and he would be sure to make it up to her some day.

"And now," cried the senator, "I want to hear it from you, am I your uncle or not?"

"You are my uncle," Karl said, then kissed his hand and was kissed on the forehead in return. "I'm very happy that I met you, but you're wrong to think that my parents only have bad things to say about you. There were also a few other mistakes in what you said, I mean, it didn't actually all happen like that. But from over here you couldn't really have got a good sense of what was going on and I don't think it's a big problem if these gentlemen have got a few incorrect details about something that can't mean very much to them."

"Well spoken," said the senator, then led Karl over to the visibly emotional captain and asked, "Don't I have a splendid nephew?"

"I'm delighted," said the captain with the kind of bow that only comes from military training, "to have met your nephew, Senator. It's a special honour for my ship to have been the place where you met. I'm just sorry to say that the crossing must have been very uncomfortable in steerage, you never know who's being carried along down there. We do everything possible to make the crossing as pleasant as possible for our steerage passengers, far more than our American counterparts, for example, but to make that journey an actual pleasure is unfortunately something we haven't yet managed."

"It hasn't done me any harm," said Karl.

"It hasn't done him any harm!" repeated the senator, laughing loudly.

"The only thing is my suitcase, which I…" and with that he remembered everything that had taken place before and that remained to be done, looked around and saw those present still standing where they'd been before, but silent with respect and amazement, their eyes directed at him. Only in the port officials, inasmuch as their stern, self-satisfied faces gave anything away, could you see regret at having come at such an inopportune time; the watch they had lying on the table was probably more important to them than everything that was happening in this room and indeed anything that could happen.

After the captain, the first to express his happiness for them was, strangely enough, the stoker. He said, "My heartiest congratulations," and shook Karl's hand, also wanting to show something like respect. But when he turned to the senator with the same phrase, the senator shifted backwards, as if the stoker were overstepping his rights, and the stoker dropped his hand at once.

The others saw what they were supposed to do and crowded around Karl and the senator. In the confusion, Karl was even offered congratulations by Schubal, which he accepted with thanks. The last to step forward were the two port officials, who said a few words in English, making a ridiculous impression.

The senator was in such a good mood that he wanted to savour every detail, and started to describe the circumstances of how this reunion had come about, something that was of course not only tolerated by the others but listened to with interest. So he told them that he'd copied the list of Karl's distinguishing features from the cook's letter into his notebook in case he needed them to hand. Then, during the stoker's unbearable waffling, he'd pulled out the notebook for no other reason than to distract himself and—just for amusement—tried to match the cook's not exactly detective-standard description to Karl's appearance. "And that's how you end up with a nephew," he concluded in a tone that made it sound as if he wanted to be congratulated again.

"What's going to happen to the stoker?" asked Karl, ignoring his uncle's latest story. In his new position he thought he was entitled to say whatever crossed his mind.

"The stoker will get whatever he deserves," said the senator, "and whatever the captain considers best. I think we've heard just about enough from the stoker, indeed more than enough, something I'm sure these gentlemen will agree with me on."

"But that's not the point, it's a question of justice," said Karl. He stood between his uncle and the captain, believing, perhaps because he was standing there, that the decision lay in his hands.

But the stoker no longer seemed to hold out any hope. He'd tucked his hands into his belt, which his agitated movements had brought into view along with part of a striped shirt. That didn't bother him in the least; he'd made his complaint, let them see what rags he wrapped around his body, and then let them carry him off. He thought that the steward and Schubal, the two lowest in rank, should be the ones to give him the final send-off. Then Schubal would be left in peace and not driven to the brink of desperation, as the chief purser had put it.

The captain would be able to hire a bunch of Romanians, everyone on board would speak Romanian and then maybe everything would indeed be better. No stoker would shoot his mouth off in the cash office and only his last tirade would be remembered, with a certain fondness, because, as the senator had said, it had prompted him to recognize his nephew. Moreover, that nephew had tried to help him several times already and so provided more than enough thanks in advance for the good turn the stoker had done him in having him recognized; it didn't occur to the stoker to now demand anything more. And anyway, he might be the nephew of a senator, but he was still a long way short of being a captain, and it was from the captain's mouth that the bad news would come. — So the stoker tried not to look at Karl, but unfortunately in this room full of enemies there was no other resting place for his eyes.

"Don't misunderstand the situation," said the senator to Karl. "It may well be a question of justice, but it's also one of discipline. Both of those things, especially the latter, are for the captain to decide."

"That's right," mumbled the stoker. Those who heard and understood smiled disconcertedly.

"Besides, we've already kept the captain from his business for long enough and it must be piling up now that he's arrived in New York. It's high time for us to leave the ship before we get unnecessarily mixed up in some petty squabble between a pair of engineers and end up turning it into more than it is. I completely understand what you're doing, by the way, my dear nephew, and that's precisely what gives me the right to lead you away from here at once."

"I'll have a boat made ready for you," said the captain, astonishing Karl by not offering the slightest objection to his uncle's self-deprecating words. The chief purser hurried over to the desk and phoned the captain's order through to the bosun.

'It's true that we're almost out of time,' Karl said to himself, 'but there's nothing I can do without insulting everybody. I can't leave my uncle when he's only just found me. The captain is polite, but no more than that. His politeness will stop when it comes to discipline, and I'm sure what my uncle said is what the captain really thinks. Schubal I don't want to talk to, I even feel bad that I shook his hand. And all the other people here are irrelevant.'

Thinking these thoughts, he slowly went over to the stoker, pulled the stoker's right hand out of his belt and held it playfully in his own. "Why don't you say anything?" he asked. "Why do you let them treat you like this?"

The stoker just wrinkled his forehead as if searching for the words to express himself.

"You've suffered an injustice, more than anyone else on this ship, I know that for sure." And Karl pulled his fingers back and forth between those of the stoker, who looked around with shining eyes, as if experiencing a moment of bliss that no one could take away from him.

"You've got to stand up for yourself, say yes and no, otherwise people won't have a clue about the truth. You've got to promise me that you'll do as I've said, because I'm very much afraid that I won't be able to help you at all any more." Karl was crying as he kissed the stoker's chapped, almost lifeless hand, pressing it against his cheek like a treasure he had to give up. — Then his uncle was at his side and, ever so gently, pulled him away.

"The stoker seems to have captivated you," he said, and looked knowingly over Karl's head at the captain. "You felt abandoned, you found the stoker and you're grateful to him, that's very commendable. But, for my sake, don't take it too far, and please start to learn your station."

Outside the office there was a sudden racket, shouting, and it even seemed as if someone was being brutally shoved against the door. A seaman came in, a little dishevelled and wearing a girl's apron. "There are people outside," he said, jabbing his elbows as if still in the ruckus. Finally he got a hold on himself and tried to salute the captain, but then noticed the apron, ripped it off, threw it on the floor and shouted, "That's disgusting! They've tied a girl's apron on me." Then he clicked his heels and saluted. Someone began to laugh, but the captain said severely, "That's what I call a good mood. Who's outside?"

"They're my witnesses," said Schubal, stepping forward. "I sincerely apologize for their behaviour. When people have a sea voyage behind them, they sometimes get a little crazy."

"Call them in right away," ordered the captain and, turning straight to the senator, he spoke politely but briskly: "If you'd be so good, Senator, as to follow this seaman with your nephew, he'll take you to the boat. I'm sure I don't have to say what a pleasure and an honour it's been to make your personal acquaintance. I only hope that we'll soon have an opportunity to carry on our conversation about the state of the American fleets, and perhaps we'll again be interrupted as pleasantly as we were today."

"One nephew's enough for the time being," said his uncle with a laugh. "And now please accept my sincerest thanks for your kindness, and I hope all goes well until we next meet. It's actually quite possible that we"—he gave Karl an affectionate squeeze—"might end up spending some time with you when we take our next trip to Europe."

"It would be a great pleasure," said the captain. The two men shook hands. Karl could only give his hand briefly and wordlessly, because the captain's attention was already consumed by the fifteen people who had trooped in, a little sheepish but still very noisy, under the supervision of Schubal. The seaman asked the senator for permission to go ahead and then cleared a way for him and Karl, who moved easily through the crowd of bowing crewmen. It seemed that these good-natured people thought of Schubal's quarrel with the stoker as a joke that even the captain could share. Among them Karl noticed the girl from the kitchens, Lina, who winked at him playfully and tied on the apron that the seaman had thrown to the floor, because it was hers.

Still following the seaman, they left the office and turned off into a narrow corridor that, after a few steps, brought them to a little door from which a short staircase led down to the boat that had been made ready for them. The seamen in the boat—into which their chief made a single, sudden leap—stood up and saluted. The senator was just giving Karl a warning to be careful going down the steps when Karl burst into painful tears. The senator took hold of Karl's chin, pressed Karl to him, and stroked his head with his other hand. In this way, step by step, they went slowly down the stairs and got into the boat, where the senator chose a good seat for Karl directly opposite himself. At a sign from the senator, the seamen pushed off from the ship and were immediately rowing hard. They were hardly a few feet from the ship when Karl noticed to his surprise that they were on the side of the ship with the windows that looked into the office. All three windows were filled with Schubal's witnesses, who waved and shouted goodbye so cheerfully that his uncle waved back and one of the seaman performed the trick of blowing a kiss off his hand without breaking the rhythm of his strokes. It was really as if the stoker didn't exist any more. Karl took a closer look at his uncle, whose knees were almost touching his own, and started to wonder whether this man could ever replace the stoker in his heart. His uncle avoided meeting his eye and looked out at the waves that were rising and falling around their boat.

GIVE UP!

I T WAS VERY EARLY in the morning, the streets clean and empty, I was going to the train station. When I compared a clock tower with the time on my watch, I saw that it was already much later than I'd thought and I really had to get a move on; the shock of this realization made me start to doubt which direction I was heading in, I didn't yet know the city very well; luckily there was a policeman nearby, I ran over to him and breathlessly asked him the way. He smiled and said, "You want me to tell you the way?"

"Yes," I said, "because I can't find it myself."

"Give up, give up," he said, and turned away abruptly, like someone who wanted to be alone with his laughter.

Translator's Acknowledgments

With thanks to Anoushiravaan Darabi,
Adam Freudenheim, Laura Macaulay
and Stella Powell-Jones.

STEFAN ZWEIG · EDGAR ALLAN POE · ISAAC BABEL
TOMÁS GONZÁLEZ · ULRICH PLENZDORF · JOSEPH KESSEL
VELIBOR ČOLIĆ · LOUISE DE VILMORIN · MARCEL AYMÉ
ALEXANDER PUSHKIN · MAXIM BILLER · JULIEN GRACQ
BROTHERS GRIMM · HUGO VON HOFMANNSTHAL
GEORGE SAND · PHILIPPE BEAUSSANT · IVÁN REPILA
E.T.A. HOFFMANN · ALEXANDER LERNET-HOLENIA
YASUSHI INOUE · HENRY JAMES · FRIEDRICH TORBERG
ARTHUR SCHNITZLER · ANTOINE DE SAINT-EXUPÉRY
MACHI TAWARA · GAITO GAZDANOV · HERMANN HESSE
LOUIS COUPERUS · JAN JACOB SLAUERHOFF
PAUL MORAND · MARK TWAIN · PAUL FOURNEL
ANTAL SZERB · JONA OBERSKI · MEDARDO FRAILE
HÉCTOR ABAD · PETER HANDKE · ERNST WEISS
PENELOPE DELTA · RAYMOND RADIGUET · PETR KRÁL
ITALO SVEVO · RÉGIS DEBRAY · BRUNO SCHULZ · TEFFI
EGON HOSTOVSKÝ · JOHANNES URZIDIL · JÓZEF WITTLIN